THE BLUE ROSE

THE
BLUE ROSE

A Collection of Stories for Girls

Edited by

Eulalie Steinmetz Ross

Illustrated by Enrico Arno

HARCOURT, BRACE & WORLD, INC., NEW YORK

The author and the publisher wish to thank the following for their
permission to use the selections reprinted in this book:

CURTIS BROWN LTD., LONDON, and DOVER PUBLICATIONS, INC., for
"The Blue Rose" by Maurice Baring from *The Art of the Story-
Teller* by Marie L. Shedlock

E. P. DUTTON & CO., INC., and J. M. DENT & SONS, LTD., for "The
Wild Swans" from *Fairy Tales* by Hans Christian Andersen,
translated by Mrs. Edgar Lucas

HARCOURT, BRACE & WORLD, INC., for "Katcha and the Devil" from
The Shepherd's Nosegay by Parker Fillmore, copyright, 1920, by
Parker Fillmore, copyright, 1948, by Louise Fillmore

HARCOURT, BRACE & WORLD, INC., and JONATHAN CAPE LIMITED for
"Gammelyn, the Dressmaker" from *Moonshine and Clover* by
Laurence Housman; and for "The Rat-Catcher's Daughter" from
A Doorway in Fairyland by Laurence Housman

HARPER & ROW for "The Princess Golden-Hair and the Great Black
Raven" from *The Wonder Clock* by Howard Pyle

HOUGHTON MIFFLIN COMPANY for "Whitebear Whittington" from
Grandfather Tales by Richard Chase. Copyright, 1948, by
Richard Chase

ALFRED A. KNOPF and THE LITERARY TRUSTEES OF WALTER DE LA
MARE and THE SOCIETY OF AUTHORS as their representative for
"Clever Grethel" from *Tales Told Again* by Walter de la Mare.
Copyright, 1927, and renewed © 1955 by Walter de la Mare

MACMILLAN & CO., LTD., for "Reflections" from *Green Willow and
Other Japanese Fairy Tales* by Grace James

HAROLD OBER ASSOCIATES for "The Seventh Princess" from *The
Little Bookroom* by Eleanor Farjeon, © 1955 by Eleanor Farjeon; and for "Nella's Dancing Shoes" from *Italian Peepshow*
by Eleanor Farjeon, copyright 1926 by Eleanor Farjeon

G. P. PUTNAM'S SONS for "The Light Princess" by George Mac-
Donald

THE VIKING PRESS, INC., for "The Princess and the Vagabone" from
The Way of the Storyteller by Ruth Sawyer. Copyright 1942 by
Ruth Sawyer

For the Youngest and the Oldest:
Caryn Allison and her great-grandfather

CONTENTS

THE BLUE ROSE

THE SEVENTH PRINCESS

from *The Little Bookroom* by Eleanor Farjeon

ID you ever hear the tale of the Six Princesses who lived for the sake of their hair alone? This is it.

There was once a King who married a Gypsy, and was as careful of her as if she had been made of glass. In case she ran away he put her in a palace in a park with a railing all round it, and never let her go outside. The Queen was too loving to tell him how much she longed to go beyond the railing, but she sat for hours on the palace roof, looking towards the meadows to the east, the river to the south, the hills to the west, and the markets to the north.

In time the Queen bore the King twin daughters as bright as the sunrise, and on the day they were christened the King in his joy asked what she would have for a gift. The Queen looked from her roof to the east, saw May on the meadows, and said:

"Give me the Spring!"

The King called fifty thousand gardeners, and bade each one bring in a root of wild-flowers or a tender birch-tree from outside, and plant it within the railing. When it was done he walked with the Queen in the flowery park, and showed her everything, saying:

"Dear wife, the Spring is yours."

But the Queen only sighed.

The following year two more Princesses, as fair as the morning, were born, and once again, on their christening-day, the King told the Queen to choose a gift. This time she looked from the roof to the south and, seeing the water shining in the valley, said:

"Give me the river!"

The King summoned fifty thousand workmen and told them so to conduct the river into the park that it should supply a most beautiful fountain in the Queen's pleasure-grounds.

Then he led his wife to the spot where the fountain rose and fell in a marble basin, and said:

"You now have the river."

But the Queen only gazed at the captive water rising and falling in its basin, and hung her head.

Next year two more Princesses, as golden as the day, were born, and the Queen, given her choice of a gift, looked north from the roof into the busy town, and said:

"Give me the people!"

So the King sent fifty thousand trumpeters down to the market-place, and before long they returned, bringing six honest market-women with them.

"Here, dear Queen, are the people," said the King.

The Queen secretly wiped her eyes, and then gave her six beautiful babies into the charge of the six buxom women, so that the Princesses had a nurse apiece.

Now in the fourth year the Queen bore only one daughter, a little one, and dark like herself, whereas the King was big and fair.

"What gift will you choose?" said the King, as they stood on the roof on the day of the christening.

The Queen turned her eyes to the west, and saw a wood-pigeon and six swans flying over the hills.

"Oh!" cried she, "give me the birds!"

The King instantly sent fifty thousand fowlers forth to snare the birds. While they were absent the Queen said:

"Dear King, my children are in their cots and I am on my throne, but presently the cots will be empty and I shall sit on my throne no more. When that day comes, which of our seven daughters will be Queen in my stead?"

Before the King could answer the fowlers returned with the birds. The King looked from the humble pigeon, with its little round head sunk in the soft breastfeathers, to the royal swans with their long white necks, and said:

"The Princess with the longest hair shall be Queen."

Then the Queen sent for the six Nurses and told them what the King had said. "So remember," she added, "to wash and brush and comb my daughters' hair without neglect, for on you will depend the future Queen."

"And who will wash and brush and comb the hair of the Seventh Princess?" they asked.

"I will do that myself," said the Queen.

Each Nurse was exceedingly anxious that her own Princess should be Queen, and every fine day they took the children out into the flowery meadow and washed their hair in the water of the fountain, and spread it in the sun to dry. Then they brushed it and combed it till it shone like yellow silk, and plaited it with ribbons, and decked it with flowers. You never saw such lovely hair as the Princesses had, or so much trouble as the Nurses took with it. And wherever the six fair girls went, the six swans went with them.

But the Seventh Princess, the little dark one, never had her hair washed in the fountain. It was kept covered with a red handkerchief, and tended in secret by the Queen as they sat together on the roof and played with the pigeon.

At last the Queen knew that her time had come. So she sent for her daughters, blessed them one by one, and bade the King carry her up to the roof. There she looked from the meadows to the river, from the markets to the hills, and closed her eyes.

Now, hardly had the King done drying his own, when a trumpet sounded at his gate, and a page came running in to say that the Prince of the World had come. So the King threw open his doors, and the Prince of the World came in, followed by his servant. The Prince was all in cloth of gold, and his mantle was so long that when he stood before the King it spread the whole length of the room, and the plume in his cap was so tall that the tip touched the ceiling. In front of the Prince walked his servant, a young man all in rags.

The King said:

"Welcome, Prince of the World!" and held out his hand.

The Prince of the World did not answer; he stood there with his mouth shut and his eyes cast down. But his Ragged Servant said, "Thank you, King of the Country!" And he took the King's hand and shook it heartily.

This surprised the King greatly.

"Cannot the Prince speak for himself?" he asked.

"If he can," said the Ragged Servant, "nobody has ever heard him do so. As you know, it takes all sorts to make the world: those who speak and those who are silent, those who are rich and those who are poor, those who think and those who do, those who look up and those who look down. Now, my master has chosen me for his servant, because between us we make up the world of which he is Prince. For he is rich and I am poor, and he thinks things and I do them, and he looks down and I look up, and he is silent, so I do the talking."

"Why has he come?" asked the King.

"To marry your daughter," said the Ragged Servant, "for it takes all sorts to make a world, and there must be a woman as well as a man."

"No doubt," said the King. "But I have seven daughters. He cannot marry them all."

"He will marry the one that is to be Queen," said the Ragged Servant.

"Let my daughters be sent for," said the King, "for the time is now come to measure the length of their hair."

So the Seven Princesses were summoned before the King. The six fair ones came in with their Nurses, and the little dark one came in by herself. The Ragged Servant looked quickly from one to another, but

the Prince of the World kept his eyes down and did
not look at any of them.

Then the King sent for the Court Tailor, with his
tape-measure; and when he came the six fair Princesses shook down their hair till it trailed on the
ground behind them.

One by one they had it measured, while the six
Nurses looked on with pride—for had they not taken
just as much care as they could of their darlings'
hair? But, alas! as neither more care nor less had
been spent upon any of them, it was now discovered
that each of the Six Princesses had hair exactly as
long as the others.

The Court held up its hands in amazement, the
Nurses wrung theirs in despair, the King rubbed his
crown, the Prince of the World kept his eyes on the
ground, and the Ragged Servant looked at the Seventh Princess.

"What shall we do," said the King, "if my youngest daughter's hair is the same length as the rest?"

"I don't think it is, sir," said the Seventh Princess,
and her sisters looked anxious as she untied the red
handkerchief from her head. And indeed her hair
was not the same length as theirs, for it was cropped
close to her head, like a boy's.

"Who cut your hair, child?" asked the King.

"My mother, if you please, sir," said the Seventh

Princess. "Every day as we sat on the roof she snipped it with her scissors."

"Well, well!" cried the King, "whichever is meant to be Queen, it isn't you!"

That is the story of the Six Princesses who lived for the sake of their hair alone. They spent the rest of their lives having it washed, brushed, and combed by the Nurses, till their locks were as white as their six pet swans.

And the Prince of the World spent the rest of *his* life waiting with his eyes cast down until one of the Princesses should grow the longest hair, and become his Queen. As this never happened, for all I know he is waiting still.

But the Seventh Princess tied on her red handkerchief again, and ran out of the palace to the hills and the river and the meadows and the markets; and the pigeon and the Ragged Servant went with her.

"But," she said, "what will the Prince of the World do without you in the palace?"

"He will have to do as best he can," said the Ragged Servant, "for it takes all sorts to make the world, those that are in and those that are out."

THE PRINCESS GOLDEN-HAIR AND
THE GREAT BLACK RAVEN

From *The Wonder Clock* by Howard Pyle

NCE upon a time there was a king who had three daughters; the two elder were handsome enough, but the youngest, whose name was Golden-Hair, was the prettiest maiden to be found within the four ends of the earth.

One day the king went out hunting with all his people. Towards evening he found himself in the forest at a place where he had never been before, and where he was not able to tell the north from the south, nor the east from the west, for he was lost. He wandered up and down and here and there, but the farther he went the less able he was to find the road home again. As he wandered thus, he came to a place where a great raven, as black as the soot in the chimney and with eyes that glowed like two coals of fire, sat in the middle of the path in front of him.

"Whither away, king?" said the Great Black Raven.

"That I cannot tell," said the king, "for I am lost."

"See now," said the Raven, "I will show you the way out of the forest, if you will give me your youngest daughter to be my wife."

"Oh, no," said the king, "I can never do such a thing as that, for my daughter is as dear to me as the apple of my eye."

"Very well, then," said the Raven, "off I go, and then there will be no getting out of the forest for you, but here you will have to stay as long as you live."

Now one will do much before one will stay in a dark forest forever, and though it was a bad piece of business to be sure, the king promised at last that if the Raven would show him the way home again, he should have the Princess Golden-Hair for his wife, though it was a pity for the girl, and that was the truth. So the Raven flapped on ahead of the king and showed him the way out of the forest.

"Tomorrow," he said, "I will come for my bride."

Sure enough, when the next morning came, there was the Great Black Raven sitting outside of the castle gateway waiting for the Princess Golden-Hair to be sent to him.

But it was not the princess whom he got after all; for the king had bade them dress the swineherd's daughter in the princess's dress, and it was she who went to the Great Black Raven. "A Great Black

Raven," said the king to himself, "will never be able to tell a swineherd's daughter from a real princess."

Well, the Raven took the swineherd's daughter on his back, and away he flew over woods and meadows, hills and valleys, until by and by he came to a rude little hut that stood on the tip top of a great bleak hill. And not a living soul was there, only a great number of birds of different kinds.

In the hut was a table, and on the table stood a golden goblet of red wine, a silver cup of white wine, and an earthenware jug full of bitter beer.

"This is our home," said the Raven; "and now will my dear one drink refreshment after her long journey?"

Yes, indeed; the swineherd's daughter would do that, for she was weary after her ride through the air. So she went to the table and took a good drink of the beer; "For," said she to herself, "the golden goblet and the silver cup are too fine for the likes of me."

Then the Raven knew that she was no true princess to be contented with bitter beer out of an earthenware jug when she could have good red wine from a golden goblet. "Come," said he, "home we go again, for you are not the bride I seek!" Therewith he took her upon his back once more, and away they flew over hill and valley till they had come back to the king's castle again.

"See," said the Raven, "this is not the one I want. Let me have my true bride or you will suffer for it."

At this the king was frightened. "Very well," said he, "come tomorrow and you shall have your true bride."

Well, when the next morning came, there was the Raven waiting outside of the castle gateway. But, after all, it was not the princess that he got, for the king had ordered that the steward's daughter should be dressed in the princess's dress; "For surely," said he to himself, "she is a good enough bride for a Great Black Raven."

So the Raven took her on his back, and away he flew till he had come to the little hut on top of the bleak hill. There stood the golden goblet, the silver cup, and the earthenware jug just as they had done before. And now would not the dear maiden drink a drop after her long journey?

Yes, indeed, that she would; so she took a good, hearty drink of the white wine in the silver cup; "For," said she to herself, "silver is none too good for a steward's daughter."

But the Raven saw very well that she was no true princess, or she would never have been contented with the silver cup. "Come," said he, "home we go again, for you are not the bride I seek." So he took her on his back once more, and away he flew to the king's castle. "See how you treat me," said he to the king; "you promise me one bride and give me another. Tomorrow morning I will come for the true one again, and if I do not get her this time, you will suffer for it, for I will pick out your eyes and tear down your castle about your ears!" And away he flew.

And now the king was terribly frightened and saw that there must be no trickery this time. So the next morning when the Raven came, it was the Princess Golden-Hair herself whom he got and none other. Up he took her on his back, and away he flew with her. As for the princess, she did nothing but weep and weep, so that when they came to the little hut on top of the bleak hill, she was glad enough to drink a drop for refreshment's sake. She never looked at the earthen jug or the silver cup, but going straight to the golden goblet, she wet her lips with the good red wine.

And then what do you think happened? Why, the hut grew and grew until it changed into a splendid castle all built of pure silver and gold, and all of the many birds outside changed into men and women servants. As for the Great Black Raven, he was a Raven no longer but the handsomest prince in all of the world, and the only thing black about him was the long curling locks of his hair. He kissed the Princess Golden-Hair and said: "Now, indeed, have I found my true bride and none other. You have freed me and my castle and all of my people from enchantment, which no one but a real princess could do, for my wicked stepmother laid spells upon us which could only be broken when a real princess drank out of the golden goblet."

Then they were married, and a fine wedding they had of it, I can tell you.

Well, a year passed by, and the princess was as happy as the days were long; but at the end of the twelve months she began to long to see her father and her sisters again. So she spoke of her longing to the Raven prince, but he only shook his head. No; he would not hear of her going, for he felt that nothing but misfortune would come of it.

But the princess begged and begged so prettily that at last the prince said she might go if she would be contented to stay only three days. Then he gave her a napkin of the finest linen and told her that whenever she wanted anything, she had only to spread the napkin and wish and it would be there. But there was one thing she must not wish for, and that was for him himself, for of that misfortune would come for sure and certain.

So off the princess went to her father's house, and

a fine sight she made of it, I can tell you; for she rode in a golden coach drawn by four milk-white horses, so that everyone she passed stopped and looked after her, and the little boys cried "Hi!" and ran along beside.

Her father and her sisters wondered what fine lady it was that was coming to the castle, and when the coach stopped, they came out to look. Dear, dear, but the king was glad to see her; as for her two sisters, they grew as green as grass with envy, for when they heard where she dwelt, and what a fine castle it was, all built of pure gold and silver, and what a handsome prince it was that she had for a husband, they were ready to burst with spite, for each felt that she might have had all this for herself if the Raven prince had only chosen her instead of Golden-Hair. So when the princess had told them all about what had happened, they only nodded and winked at one another as though they did not believe a word of it.

"Yes, yes," said they, "it is all very well to talk about your handsome prince; but why did he not come along with you, we should like to know?"

The princess could not tell them that; but she could bring him quickly enough whenever she chose, for all that she had to do was to spread her napkin and wish and he would be there. She would show them that what she had said was true, had her prince not forbidden her.

But the envious sisters only jeered and laughed as though all that the princess said was the best jest in the world.

Now one can bear anything better than laughter. So the end of the matter was that the princess spread the linen napkin on the floor and wished that the Raven prince might be with them.

No sooner had she wished it than there he stood; but he looked at no one but her. "Did I not tell you that misfortune would come of it if you wished for me?" said he. "Now, I must leave you and go where you are not likely ever to see me again."

Then the princess would have spoken, but he gave her no time for that. He snatched up the napkin, and becoming a Raven once more, he flew through the open window and across the tree-tops and was gone. At the same time her golden coach vanished, and the coachman and footmen became so many birds and flew away, so that not one of her fine things was left.

The poor princess wept and cried for a whole day and a whole night. But at the end of that time she dried her eyes and, tucking up her skirts, started off into the wide world to find her dear prince again.

Well, she travelled on and on and on for more days than she could count, and till she had been over nearly all of the world, but in all that time she could learn no news of the prince nor of whither he had gone. At last one day, about nightfall, she came to a little hut in a deep forest, and in the hut sat an old woman with hair as white as snow.

"What do you want, child?" said the old woman. "Do you not know that this is Death's house, and that if he returns and finds you here, he will kill you? I tell you that he spares neither the young nor the old, the plain nor the handsome. As for me, I am his grand-mother."

But all this was one to the princess, and went in at one ear and out at the other; she could no longer drag one foot after the other, so there she must stay even if Death should find her when he came home.

Then she told Death's grandmother all that had happened to her, and Death's grandmother took pity on her because she was so pretty and so tired. She gave the princess something to eat and then hid her in the tall clock that stood in the corner, so that Death might not find her when he came home.

By and by in came Death and hung up his great scythe behind the door. "Hu-u-u-u!" cried he, "I smell Christian blood in the house for sure."

"Christian blood, indeed!" said his grandmother.

"As though a Christian would come to this house if he had anywhere else to go! But now I think of it, a crow flew overhead today and dropped a bone down the chimney. I threw it out as soon as I could, but perhaps that is what you smell."

So Death said nothing more, but sat down to supper and ate heartily, for he had had a long journey that day.

"See," said his grandmother, "I had a dream to-day. A princess is out in the world hunting for her Raven sweetheart and cannot tell where to find him."

"That is easy enough to tell," said Death; "he lives in a great castle that stands at the end of the earth on a high hill of smooth glass."

"That is good," said Death's grandmother, "but I dreamed that after she found where he lived, she was too weary to journey thither."

"That is easy enough, too," said Death; "out in the forest yonder stands my pale horse tied to an oak-tree. If she could only find the horse and loose the bridle and mount his back, he would take her there quickly enough, for he can travel more rapidly than the north wind."

"Yes, yes, that is all very well," said Death's grand-mother, "but I had a third dream. I thought that when she came to the smooth hill of glass, she did not know how to climb to the top; what is the answer to that?"

"Prut!" said Death, "that is easy to tell. Over by the glass hill are seven birds fighting in the tree-top for an old hat. If she will throw a stone in the midst of them, they will drop the hat and fly away. It is Wish's own hat, and if she will put it on her head and wish herself at the top of the hill, she will be there quickly enough, I can tell you."

After that Death put on his cloak and took up his scythe and was off like a whirlwind, for he has little time to spare for talking, folks say. Then Death's grandmother opened the clock, and the princess came out and thanked her and went her way.

She hunted here and there through the forest until, sure enough, she found Death's great pale horse tied to an oak-tree. She loosened the bridle and mounted upon his back, and away they went till the chips and the stones flew behind them. So they soon came to the high hill of smooth glass that stood at the end of the earth, and there, on top of it, was the castle of the prince.

The princess dismounted from the pale horse, and away he galloped home again.

Then the princess hunted for the birds that Death said fought for Wish's hat, and presently she heard them making a great hubbub and, looking up, saw them in the tree-top above her, fighting for the old hat, just as Death said they would be doing. She picked up a stone and threw it in the midst of them, and they dropped the hat and flew away screaming. Then she put on the hat and wished herself at the top of the hill, and there she was as quick as a wink.

Now, her shoes were worn into holes by long journeying, and her clothes were torn to threads and tatters by the brambles through which she had passed and hung fluttering all about her, and she looked for all the world like nothing else than a common beggar-maid, except for her golden hair. So it was that when she knocked at the door of the prince's castle and the porter came and opened it and heard that she wanted to see the prince, he snapped his fingers and laughed. All the same he told her that the cook wanted a serving wench in the kitchen and that she might have the place if she liked; if that did not suit her, she might be jogging the way that she had come.

Well, there was nothing for it but for the princess to serve in the kitchen or to go away again. So she bound up her hair in a tattered kerchief so that the beautiful golden tresses might not be seen, and down she went to serve the cook.

The prince's dinner was cooking at the fire, and the princess was to watch it so that it might not be burned. So she watched it, and as she watched it she wept.

"Why do you weep, hussy?" said the cook.

"Ah me!" said the princess. "Once I ate with my love and drank with my love and lived by his side. If he did but know to what I have come, how his heart would ache!"

After that the dinner was served, but while nobody was looking, the princess plucked a strand of her golden hair and laid it upon a white napkin and the napkin upon an empty plate. Over all she placed a silver cover, and when the Raven prince lifted it, there lay the strand of golden hair. "Where did this come from?" said he. But nobody could tell him that.

The next day the same thing happened; the princess watched the dinner, and as she watched she wept.

"Why do you weep, hussy?" said the cook. And thereto the princess answered as she had done before: "Ah me! Once I ate with my love and drank with my love and lived by his side. If he did but know to what I have come, how his heart would ache!"

Then, while nobody was looking, she plucked another strand of golden hair, and the prince found it as he had done the other, and no one could tell him whence it came.

The third day the same thing happened as had happened twice before: the princess watched and wept and, when nobody was looking, plucked a third strand of golden hair and sent it to the prince as she had the others.

Then the prince sent for the cook. "Who has been serving this and that with my dinner?" said he.

The cook shook his head, for he knew nothing, but perhaps the new serving wench could tell, for she wept and said things that none of them understood. When the prince heard this, he sent for her, and the princess came and stood before him. He looked at her and knew her, for her golden hair shone through a hole in the ugly headdress that she wore. Then he reached out his hand and snatched it off of her head, and her golden hair fell down all about her shoulders until it reached the floor. Then he took her in his arms and kissed her, and that was the end of all of her troubles.

After that they had a grand time at the castle; everyone who came had all that he could eat, and wine and beer flowed like water. I, too, was there, but I brought nothing away with me in my pockets.

CLEVER GRETHEL

from *Tales Told Again* by Walter de la Mare

HERE was once a cook, and her name was Grethel. She wore shoes with red rosettes on them, and when she went walking in these shoes she would turn herself this way and that, saying: "Well I never, you *are* a handsome creature!"

At night as she combed her hair in the glass she would say: "My! so there you are!" And they called her "clever Grethel."

Whenever after a walk she came home to her master's house again, she would always take a little sippet of wine. "You see, Grethel, my dear, it makes the tongue able to *taste* better," she would say. "And what's a cook without a tongue?" In fact, Grethel kept her tongue very busy, nibbling and tasting.

Now one day her master said to her: "I have a guest coming this evening, Grethel, and a guest that knows what's what, and I want you to roast us a pair of fowls for supper. Two, mind you, young and tender. And I want 'em roasted to a turn."

Grethel said: "Why, yes, master. They shall taste so good you won't know what you're eating."

So she killed two fowls, scalded and plucked them, tucked in their legs with a little bit of liver in between, stuffed them with stuffing, and towards evening put them down to a clear, red fire to roast. She basted and basted them, and when they were done to a turn and smelt sweet as Arabia, and their breasts were a rich, clear, delicate brown, Grethel called out to her master:

"If that guest of yours don't come soon, master, I shall have to take the fowls away from the fire. And I warn you, they will be utterly spoilt, for they are just at their juiciest."

Her master said: "So, so! I will run out and see if he is coming."

As soon as her master had turned his back, Grethel thought to herself she would have another sip of something to drink. Having had one sip, she took another sip, and then another. Then she basted the fowls again, and twisted the spit. She puffed with the heat, the fire blazing in her face. Suddenly, as she stood looking at the fowls, she thought to herself: "Now cooking's cooking! I shouldn't wonder if them birds taste as good as they smell. Oh, oh, oh! It's a sin. It's a shame!"

Then she looked out of the window; and when she saw that nobody was coming, she said to herself: "There! what did I tell you? And lawks! one of the wings is burning." So she cut off the wing with a twist of her sharp knife, and holding it between her finger and thumb, ate every scrap of it up, to the very bone.

Then, "Dear me," she sighed to herself, looking at the chicken, "that one wing left looks like another wing missing!" So she ate up the other. Then she took another sip of wine, and once more looked at the fowls.

"Now think what a sad thing," she said. "Once those two poor hens were sisters, and you couldn't tell 'em apart. But now look at them: one whole and the other nowt but legs!" So she gobbled up the wings of the other chicken to make the pair look more alike. And still her master did not come. Then said she to herself:

"Lor', Grethel, my dear, why worry? There won't be any guest to-night. He has forgotten all about it. And master can have some nice dry bread and cheese." With that she ate up completely one of the chickens, skin, stuffing, gravy and all, and then, see-ing how sad and lonely the other looked all by itself with its legs sticking up in the air and both its wings gone, she finished off that too.

She was picking the very last sweet morsel off its wishbone when her master came running into the kitchen, and cried: "Quick, Grethel! Dish up! dish up! Our guest has just turned the corner."

At this moment she was standing in front of the fire in her fine shoes and great cooking apron, and she looked over her shoulder at her master. But he at once rushed out to see if the table was ready, and the wine on it, snatched up the great carving-knife, and began to sharpen it on the doorstep.

Pretty soon after, the guest came to the door and knocked. Grethel ran softly out, caught him by the sleeve, pushed him out of the porch, pressed her finger on her lips, and whispered: "Ssh! Ssh! on your life! Listen, now, and be off I beseech you! My poor master has gone clean out of his senses at your being so late. Mad! mad! If he catches you, he will cut your ears off. Hark now! He is sharpening his knife on the doorstep!"

At this the guest turned pale as ashes, and hearing the steady rasping of the knife on the stone, ran off down the street as fast as his legs could carry him. As soon as he was out of sight, Grethel hastened back to her master.

"La, master!" she said, "*you've* asked a nice fine guest to supper!"

"Why," says he, looking up with the knife in his hand, "what's wrong with him?"

"Wrong!" says she. "Why, he had scarce put his nose in at the door, when he gives a sniff. 'What! chicken!' says he, 'roast chicken!' And away he rushed into the kitchen, snatched up my two poor beeeootiful birds, and without even waiting for the dish or the gravy, ran off with them down the street."

"What, *now?*" said her master.

"This very minute!" said Grethel.

"Both?" said her master.

"Both," said she.

"Heaven save us!" said her master. "Then I shall have nothing for supper!" And off he ran in chase of his guest, as fast as he could pelt, crying out as he did so:

"Hi, there! Stop! Stop! Hi! Just one! Just one! Only one!"

But the guest, hearing these words, and supposing that the madman behind him with his long knife meant one of his ears, ran on faster than ever into the darkness of the night.

And Grethel sat down, happy and satisfied. She gave one deep sigh, looked solemnly at the two bright red rosettes on her shoes, and had another sip or two of wine.

THE RAT-CATCHER'S DAUGHTER

from *A Doorway in Fairyland* by Laurence Housman

ONCE upon a time there lived an old rat-catcher who had a daughter, the most beautiful girl that had ever been born. Their home was a dirty little cabin; but they were not so poor as they seemed, for every night the rat-catcher took the rats he had cleared out of one house and let them go at the door of another, so that on the morrow he might be sure of a fresh job.

His rats got quite to know him, and would run to him when he called; people thought him the most wonderful rat-catcher, and could not make out how it was that a rat remained within reach of his operations.

Now anyone can see that a man who practiced so cunning a roguery was greedy beyond the intentions of Providence. Every day, as he watched his daughter's beauty increase, his thoughts were: "When will she be able to pay me back for all the expense she has been to me?" He would have grudged her the very food she ate, if it had not been necessary to keep her in the good looks which were some day to bring him his fortune. For he was greedier than any gnome after gold.

Now all good gnomes have this about them: they love whatever is beautiful, and hate to see harm happen to it. A gnome who lived far away underground, below where stood the rat-catcher's house, said to his fellows: "Up yonder is a man who has a daughter; so greedy is he, he would sell her to the first comer who gave him gold enough! I am going up to look after her."

So one night, when the rat-catcher set a trap, the gnome went and got himself caught in it. There in the morning, when the rat-catcher came, he found a funny little fellow, all bright and golden, wriggling and beating to be free.

"I can't get out!" cried the little gnome. "Let me go!"

The rat-catcher screwed up his mouth to look virtuous. "If I let you out, what will you give me?"

"A sack full of gold," answered the gnome, "just as heavy as myself—not a pennyweight less!"

"Not enough!" said the rat-catcher. "Guess again!"

"As heavy as you are!" cried the gnome, beginning to plead in a thin, whining tone.

"I'm a poor man," said the rat-catcher; "a poor man mayn't afford to be generous!"

"What is it you want of me?" cried the gnome.

"If I let you go," said the rat-catcher, "you must make me the richest man in the world!" Then he thought of his daughter: "Also you must make the king's son marry my daughter; then I will let you go."

The gnome laughed to himself to see how the trapper was being trapped in his own avarice as, with the most melancholy air, he answered: "I can make you the richest man in the world; but I know of no way of making the king's son marry your daughter, except one."

"What way?" asked the rat-catcher.

"Why," answered the gnome, "for three years your daughter must come and live with me underground, and by the end of the third year her skin will be changed into pure gold like ours. And do you know any king's son who would refuse to marry a beautiful maiden who was pure gold from the sole of her foot to the crown of her head?"

The rat-catcher had so greedy an inside that he could not believe in any king's son refusing to marry a maiden of pure gold. So he clapped hands on the bargain, and let the gnome go.

The gnome went down into the ground, and fetched up sacks and sacks of gold, until he had made the rat-catcher the richest man in the world. Then the father called his daughter, whose name was Jasomé, and bade her follow the gnome down into the heart of the earth.

It was all in vain that Jasomé begged and implored; the rat-catcher was bent on having her married to the king's son. So he pushed, and the gnome pulled, and down she went; and the earth closed after her.

The gnome brought her down to his home under the hill upon which stood the town. Everywhere round her were gold and precious stones; the very air was full of gold dust, so that when she remained still it settled on her hands and her hair, and a soft golden down began to show itself over her skin. So there in the house of the gnomes sat Jasomé and cried; and, far away overhead, she heard the days come and go, by the sound of people walking and the rolling of wheels.

The gnome was very kind to her; nothing did he spare of underground commodities that might afford her pleasure. He taught her the legends of all the heroes that have gone down into earth and been forgotten, and the lost songs of the old poets, and the buried languages that once gave wisdom to the world: down there all these things are remembered.

She became the most curiously accomplished and wise maiden that ever was hidden from the light of day. "I have to train you," said the gnome, "to be fit for a king's bride!" But Jasomé, though she thanked him, only cried to be let out.

In front of the rat-catcher's house rose a little spring of salt water with gold dust in it, that gilded the basin where it sprang. When he saw it, he began rubbing his hands with delight, for he guessed well enough that his daughter's tears had made it; and the dust in it told him how surely now she was being turned into gold.

And now the rat-catcher was the richest man in the world: all his traps were made of gold, and when he went rat-hunting he rode in a gilded coach drawn by twelve hundred of the finest and largest rats. This was for an advertisement of the business. He now caught rats for the fun of it, and the show of it, but also to get money by it; for though he was so rich, ratting and money-grubbing had become a second nature to him; unless he were at one or the other, he could not be happy.

Far below, in the house of the gnome, Jasomé sat and cried. When the sound of the great bells ringing for Easter came down to her the gnome said: "Today I cannot bind you; it is the great rising day for all Christians. If you wish, you may go up and ask your father now to release you."

So Jasomé kissed the gnome, and went up the track of her own tears, that brought her to her father's door. When she came to the light of day, she felt quite blind; a soft yellow tint was all over her, and already her hair was quite golden.

The rat-catcher was furious when he saw her coming back before her time. "Oh, father," she cried, "let me come back for a little while to play in the sun!" But her father, fearing lest the gilding of her complexion should be spoiled, drove her back into the earth, and trampled it down over her head.

The gnome seemed quite sorry for her when she returned; but already, he said, a year was gone—and what were three years, when a king's son would be the reward?

At the next Easter he let her go again; and now she looked quite golden, except for her eyes, and her white teeth, and the nails on her pretty little fingers and toes. But again her father drove her back into the ground, and put a heavy stone slab over the spot to make sure of her.

At last the third Easter came, and she was all gold.

She kissed the gnome many times, and was almost sorry to leave him, for he had been very kind to her.

And now he told her about her father's catching him in the trap, and robbing him of his gold by a hard bargain, and of his being forced to take her down to live with him till she was turned into gold, so that she might marry the king's son. "For now," said he, "you are so compounded of gold that only the gnomes could rub it off you."

So this time, when Jasomé came up once more to the light of day, she did not go back again to her cruel father, but went and sat by the roadside, and played with the sunbeams, and wondered when the king's son would come and marry her.

And as she sat there all the country-people who passed by stopped and mocked her; and boys came and threw mud at her because she was all gold from head to foot—an object, to be sure, for all simple folk to laugh at. So presently, instead of hoping, she fell to despair, and sat weeping, with her face hidden in her hands.

Before long the king's son came along that road, and saw something shining like sunlight on a pond; but when he came near, he found a lovely maiden of pure gold lying in a pool of her own tears, with her face hidden in her hair.

Now the king's son, unlike the country-folk, knew the value of gold; but he was grieved at heart for a maiden so stained all over with it, and more, when he beheld how she wept. So he went to lift her up; and there, surely, he saw the most beautiful face he could ever have dreamed of. But, alas! so discoloured—even her eyes, and her lips, and the very tears she shed were the colour of gold! When he could bring her to speak, she told him how, because she was all gold, all the people mocked at her, and boys threw mud at her; and she had nowhere to go, unless it were back to the kind gnome who lived underground, out of sight of the sweet sun.

So the prince said, "Come with me, and I will take you to my father's palace, and there nobody shall mock you, but you shall sit all your days in the sunshine and be happy."

And as they went, more and more he wondered at her great beauty—so spoiled that he could not look at her without grief—and was taken with increasing wonder at the beautiful wisdom stored in her golden mind; for she told him the tales of the heroes which she had learned from the gnome, and of buried cities; also the songs of old poets that have been forgotten; and her voice, like the rest of her, was golden.

The prince said to himself, "I shut my eyes, and am ready to die loving her; yet, when I open them, she is but a talking statue!"

One day he said to her, "Under all this disguise

you must be the most beautiful thing upon earth! Already to me you are the dearest!" and he sighed, for he knew that a king's son might not marry a figure of gold.

Now one day after this, as Jasomé sat alone in the sunshine and cried, the little old gnome stood before her, and said, "Well, Jasomé, have you married the king's son?"

"Alas!" cried Jasomé, "you have so changed me: I am no longer human! Yet he loves me, and, but for that, he would marry me."

"Dear me!" said the gnome. "If that is all, I can take the gold off you again: why, I said so!"

Jasomé entreated him, by all his former kindness, to do so for her now.

"Yes," said the gnome, "but a bargain is a bargain. Now is the time for me to get back my bags of gold. Do you go to your father, and let him know that the king's son is willing to marry you if he restores to me my treasure that he took from me; for that is what it comes to."

Up jumped Jasomé, and ran to the rat-catcher's house. "Oh, father," she cried, "now you can undo all your cruelty to me; for now, if you will give back the gnome his gold, he will give my own face back to me, and I shall marry the king's son!"

But the rat-catcher was filled with admiration at

the sight of her, and would not believe a word she
said. "I have given you your dowry," he answered;
"three years I had to do without you to get it. Take
it away and get married, and leave me the peace and
plenty I have so hardly earned!"

Jasomé went back and told the gnome. "Really,"
said he, "I must show this rat-catcher that there are
other sorts of traps, and that it isn't only rats and
gnomes that get caught in them! I have given him
his taste of wealth; now it shall act as pickle to his
poverty!"

So the next time the rat-catcher put his foot out of
doors the ground gave way under it, and, snap!—the
gnome had him by the leg.

"Let me go!" cried the rat-catcher; "I can't get
out!"

"Can't you?" said the gnome. "If I let you out,
what will you give me?"

"My daughter!" cried the rat-catcher; "my beautiful golden daugher!"

"Oh no!" laughed the gnome. "Guess again!"

"My own weight in gold!" cried the rat-catcher,
in a frenzy; but the gnome would not close the bargain till he had wrung from the rat-catcher the
promise of his last penny.

So the gnome carried away all the sacks of gold
before the rat-catcher's eyes; and when he had them

safe underground, then at last he let the old man go. Then he called Jasomé to follow him, and she went down willingly into the black earth.

For a whole year the gnome rubbed and scrubbed and tubbed her to get the gold out of her composition; and when it was done, she was the most shiningly beautiful thing you ever set eyes on.

When she got back to the palace, she found her dear prince pining for love of her, and wondering when she would return. So they were married the very next day; and the rat-catcher came to look on at the wedding.

He grumbled because he was in rags, and because he was poor; he wept that he had been robbed of his money and his daughter. But gnomes and daughters, he said, were in one and the same box; such ingratitude as theirs no one could beat.

THE WILD SWANS

edited by the compiler from Hans Christian Andersen's *Fairy Tales*, translated by Mrs. Edgar Lucas

FAR away, where the swallows take refuge in winter, lived a king who had eleven sons and one daughter, Elise. The eleven brothers were all princes, and they went to school with stars on their breasts and swords at their sides. They wrote upon golden slates with diamond pencils, and could read just as well without a book as with one, so there was no mistake about their being princes. Their sister Elise sat upon a footstool of looking-glass, and she had a picture book which cost half a kingdom. Oh, these children were very happy; but it was not to be this way forever.

Their father, who was king over all the land, married a wicked queen who was not at all kind to the poor children. They found that out the first day. All was festive in the castle to celebrate the wedding, and the children wanted to play at having company too. But instead of having as many cakes and baked apples as ever they wanted, the new queen would only allow them sand in their tea-cups and said they must make-believe with it.

The next week she sent little Elise into the country to live with a peasant family, and it did not take her long to make the king believe so many wicked tales about the boys that he cared no more about them.

Then the queen, who possessed magical powers, pronounced an enchantment over the eleven young princes. "Fly away like big birds without voices," she said. "Fly out into the world and look after yourselves."

But the queen could not make things as bad for them as she would have liked, for the princes turned into eleven beautiful wild swans. With a strange cry they flew out of the palace window, across the park, and disappeared in the woods.

It was very early morning when they came to the place in the wood where their sister Elise was sleeping in the peasants' house. They hovered over the roof of the house, turning and twisting their long necks and flapping their great wings. But no one either saw or heard them. Then they soared up towards the clouds, for they had to fly away again far out into the wide world. Later they settled in a great, dark forest that stretched down to the shores of the sea.

Poor little Elise stayed in the peasants' hut, and one day passed like another. She played with a green leaf, for she had no other toys. She pricked a little hole in the leaf, which she looked through at the sun. It seemed to her then that she saw her brothers' bright eyes. And when the warm sunbeams shone upon her cheeks, it reminded her of their kisses.

As the years passed, Elise grew as beautiful as she was good. When the wind tossed the rose-hedge outside the peasants' house, it whispered to the roses, "Who can be prettier than you?" But the roses shook their heads and answered, "Elise!" And when the old woman sat in the doorway reading her prayer book, the wind turned over the leaves and said to the book, "Who can be more pious than you?" "Elise!" answered the book. And both the roses and the prayer book spoke the truth.

Elise went home when she was fifteen, but when the queen saw how beautiful the princess had become, she was angry and her heart filled with hatred. She would gladly have turned Elise into a wild swan too, like her brothers, but she did not dare, for the king wished to see his daughter. So the queen devised another plan.

Early in the morning the queen went to the bath that was built of white marble. She took three toads, kissed them, and said to the first:

"Sit upon Elise's head when she comes to the bath so that she may become stupid like yourself."

"Sit upon her forehead," she said to the second, "that she may become ugly like you and her father won't recognize her!"

"Rest upon her heart," she whispered to the third. "Let an evil spirit come into her and give her pain."

Thereupon the queen put the toads into the clean water, and at once it turned green. Then she called Elise and made her go into the bath. When Elise went down into the water, one of the toads fastened itself in her hair, another sat upon her forehead, and the third clung to her heart. But when the princess stood up, three scarlet poppies floated on the water —the toads had become flowers from just having rested a moment on her head and her heart. She was too good and innocent for sorcery to have any power over her.

When the wicked queen saw this, she tried yet another scheme. She rubbed Elise all over with walnut juice, smeared her face with evil-smelling salve, and tousled her beautiful hair. No one could have recognized the princess, and when her father saw her, he was quite horrified and said she could not possibly be his daughter. Only the watch dog and the swallows knew her, and they were poor dumb creatures who had nothing to say in the matter.

Poor Elise crept sadly out of the palace and wandered about all day over meadows and marshes and, at last, into a great forest. She did not know in the least where she was going; she only wept as she went and longed for her brothers, whom she judged to have been driven out of the palace like herself.

She made up her mind then to go and look for them. But she had been in the wood for a short time when night fell, so she lay down upon the soft moss and rested her head on a little hillock. The air was mild in the forest, and it was very still. Hundreds of glow-worms shone around her like green fire in the grass. When she gently moved one of the branches over her head, the little shining insects fell over her like a shower of stars. And all night long she dreamed about her brothers.

When she woke, the sun was already high and there was a fresh scent of grass and herbs in the air. She could hear the splashing of water nearby, and by following a path the deer had made, Elise came upon a pond with a lovely sandy bottom. The water was so clear that, had not the branches of the trees moved in the wind, she would have thought them painted on the bottom of the pond, so plainly was every leaf reflected.

When Elise stooped to drink, the clear water reflected her own face like a mirror, and she was quite frightened. But when she wet her hand and rubbed her forehead and her cheeks, her white skin shone through again. Then she laid aside her clothes and went into the fresh water and washed away the walnut stain and the evil-smelling salve. When she was dressed again and had plaited her long hair, a more beautiful royal princess than she could not be found in all the world.

After she had drunk of a sparkling spring that fed the pool, Elise wandered on further into the woods, though she had not the least idea where she was going. Presently she met an old woman with a basket full of berries, and the old woman gave some of them to the princess, and they served for her breakfast. Elise asked the old woman if she had seen eleven princes riding through the woods.

"No," said the old woman, "but yesterday I saw eleven swans, with golden crowns upon their heads, swimming in a stream close by here."

She led Elise up a hill at the foot of which a stream ran. Elise thanked the old woman, said good-by to her, and walked along the stream until it flowed into the sea.

Before the princess lay the beautiful open sea, but not a sail was to be seen on it, not a single boat. How was she to get any further in her search for her brothers? Then she saw eleven white swans' feathers lying on the seaweed, and she picked them up and held them as a token—and for courage—through the long day.

When the sun was just about to go down, Elise saw eleven wild swans with golden crowns upon their heads flying toward the shore. They flew, one behind the other, like a white ribbon streamer. Lest she frighten them, Elise climbed up a bank and hid behind a bush. The swans settled close by her and flapped their great white wings.

And as soon as the sun had sunk beneath the water, the swans threw off their feathers, and there stood eleven handsome princes. They were Elise's brothers, and although they had changed a great deal, she knew them at once. She came from behind the bush calling their names and rushed into their arms. They knew her, too, for all that she had grown so tall and beautiful. They laughed and cried and told each other how wickedly the queen had treated them all.

"We brothers," said the oldest, "have to fly about in the form of swans as long as the sun is above the horizon. When it goes down, we regain our human shapes. Near sunset, then, we always have to look for a resting place, for should we happen to be flying up among the clouds when the sun goes down, we

should be hurled to the earth below. We are not permitted to live here in our homeland; we are in exile in another land, just as beautiful as this, beyond the sea. The way to it is long, and we have to cross the mighty ocean to get to it. We are permitted to visit the home of our father once a year, and we dare stay only eleven days. We must make the trip during the longest days of the year, for the flight takes two days and there is not a single island on the way where we can spend the night. Only one solitary rock juts up above the water midway, and it is just big enough for us to stand upon, close together; and if there is a heavy sea, the water splashes us. There we stay overnight in our human forms and fly on when the sun comes up, as wild swans. Tomorrow we must fly away again across the ocean, and we dare not come back for a whole year. But we can't leave you here like this. Yet how can we take you with us? We have neither ship nor boat!"

When the eldest brother had ceased speaking, the youngest spoke up. "Surely, brother, the wings of all of us ought to be strong enough to carry our sister across the ocean. Have you courage to go with us, Elise?"

"Oh, yes," said the princess. "Take me with you!"

The brothers and sister spent the whole night weaving a kind of net from pliant willow bark bound together with tough rushes. They made it large and they made it strong, and when it was finished, Elise lay down upon it and went to sleep. When the sun rose and the brothers became swans again, they took up the net in their bills and flew high up among the clouds with their precious sister who was still fast asleep. The sunbeams fell straight onto her face, so the swan who was the youngest brother flew over her head to shade her with his wide wings.

They were far from land when Elise woke; she thought she must still be dreaming, so strange did it seem to be carried through the air high above the sea. They were so high that the first ship they saw looked like a gull floating on the water. A great cloud came up behind them like a mountain, and Elise saw the shadow of herself on it, and those of the eleven swans looking like giants.

The swans flew on and on all day, cleaving through the air like an arrow, but still they went more slowly than usual because they had their sister to carry. A storm came up and night was drawing on. Elise saw the sun sinking with terror in her heart, for the solitary rock was nowhere to be seen. As soon as the sun went down, the swans would become men again, and they would all be hurled into the sea and drowned. The black clouds gathered, strong gusts of wind came with the storm, and flashes of lightning followed it.

The sun was now at the edge of the sea, and the swans shot downwards so suddenly Elise thought they were falling and her heart quaked. But then she saw, for the first time, the little rock thrusting out of the water and looking no bigger than the head of a seal. Now the sun was half below the horizon, sinking very quickly. It was no bigger than a star when Elise's foot touched the rock, and it went out like the last spark on a bit of burning paper as her brothers cast off their swan feathers and stood arm in arm around the princess. The waves beat on the rock and washed over Elise and her brothers like drenching rain. The sky shone with continuous lightning, and the thunder rolled, peal upon peal. But the sister and brothers were together, and they gave courage and comfort to each other.

At last the night and the storm were past, and the air at dawn was pure and still. As soon as the sun rose, the swans flew off with Elise. Constant changes passed before the princess's eyes that day made from clouds and sea mist and the mighty roar of the ocean. And then she saw the real land where she was to live with her brothers. Beautiful blue mountains rose before her with cedar woods and golden palaces. Long before the sun went down, she sat among the hills in front of a great cave covered with green creepers.

"Now we shall see what you will dream here to-night," said the youngest brother as he showed her where she was to sleep.

"If only I might dream how to free you from your enchantment," said Elise. This thought filled her mind and heart when she went to sleep. And in her sleep she seemed to be flying up to a castle in the air. A fairy came toward her; she was fair and shining, and yet she looked very like the old woman who had given Elise the berries in the wood and told her about the swans with the golden crowns.

"Your brothers can be set free," said the fairy, "but have you courage and endurance enough for it? Do you see this stinging nettle I hold in my hand? Many of this kind grow round the cave where you sleep; only these and the ones which grow in the churchyards may be used. Remember that! These you must gather, although they will burn and blister your hands. Crush the nettles with your feet and you will have flax, and of this you must weave eleven coats of mail with long sleeves. Throw these over the eleven wild swans and the enchantment is broken! But remember, from the moment you begin your task till it is finished, even if it takes years, you must not utter a word! The first word you say will fall like a dagger into the hearts of your brothers. Their lives are at the mercy of your tongue. Mark this well!"

Then the fairy touched Elise's hand with the nettle; it was like burning fire and the princess woke. It was bright daylight, and close to where she slept lay a nettle like those in her dream. Elise hurried out of the cave to begin her task.

She seized the horrid nettles with her delicate hands, and they burnt like fire. Great blisters rose on her hands and arms, but she suffered them gladly if only she might free her beloved brothers. She crushed every nettle with her bare feet, and then twisted them into green flax.

When the brothers returned at sunset, they were alarmed because their sister did not speak to them. They feared this was some new witchcraft of the wicked queen. But when they saw the princess's hands, they understood that it was for their sakes that she was silent, and that she labored. The youngest brother wept, and where his tears fell on Elise's hands and feet, the blisters disappeared and the pain was no more.

The princess spent the whole night at her work; and all the following day while her brothers were away she sat solitary, but never had the time flown so fast. One shirt of mail was finished, and she began the next. Then a hunting-horn sounded among the mountains. Elise was much frightened. The sound came nearer, and was joined by the barking of dogs. In terror Elise rushed into the cave, tied the nettles she had collected and woven into a bundle, and sat upon it as if to protect it.

Presently a dog bounded from the thicket, and another and another. They barked loudly and ran backward and forward before the cave. Soon the huntsmen were at the entrance of the cave. The handsomest of these was the king of the country. He entered the cave and stood in astonishment before Elise. He had never seen so lovely a girl.

"How come you here, child?" asked the king.

Elise shook her head; she dared not speak for the lives of her brothers depended upon her silence.

"You shall come with me," said the king. "You cannot stay here. If you are as good as you are beautiful, I shall dress you in silks and velvets, put a golden crown upon your head, and you shall live with me in my finest palace!"

Elise wept and wrung her hands, but the king lifted her before him on his horse and started back across the mountains to his castle, and the huntsmen followed.

When the sun went down, the royal city lay before

them. The king led Elise into the palace, where great fountains played in marble halls and walls and ceilings were covered with paintings. But Elise had eyes for none of them; she only wept and sorrowed. The ladies-in-waiting dressed her in royal robes, twisted pearls into her hair, and drew gloves onto her blistered hands.

She was dazzlingly lovely as she stood there in all her magnificence. The courtiers bowed low before her, and the king ordered all the church bells to ring marriage peals. The beautiful mute girl from the forest was to be queen of the land. The chancellor shook his head and whispered that he feared the beautiful wood maiden was a witch who had dazzled their eyes and stolen the heart of their king. The king refused to listen to him, the wedding took place, and the chancellor himself had to put the crown upon the new queen's head.

Then the king ordered the music to play, the richest food to be brought, and the loveliest girls to dance before his bride. She was led through scented gardens into beautiful rooms, but nothing brought a smile to her lips or into her eyes. Sorrow had set its seal upon them. At length the king opened the door of a small room connected to the royal bedchamber. It was covered with costly green carpets and made to look exactly like the cave where he had found Elise. On the floor lay the bundle of flax she had spun from the nettles, and from the ceiling hung the shirt of mail which was already finished.

"Here you may dream you are back in your cave," said the king. "Here is the work you were doing, and in the midst of your splendors now it may amuse you to think of those other times."

When Elise saw all these things so precious to her, a smile for the first time played upon her lips and the blood rushed back to her cheeks. The hope that she could still free her brothers returned to her, and she kissed the king's hand in gratitude. Her lips were still sealed, but her eyes were full of love for the good and handsome king who did everything he could to please her. Every day she grew more and more fond of him and longed to confide in him and tell him of her sufferings; but silent she must remain, and in silence bring her labors to completion.

Therefore, at night Elise stole away from the side of the king to the little room which resembled the cave, and there she knitted one shirt of mail after another. But when she came to the seventh shirt, all the flax was gone. She remembered that the nettles she used to make the flax grew in churchyards, and she remembered she had to gather them herself. But how was she to get to a churchyard? With a trembling heart she stole out of the palace into the moonlit garden, and then crept through long alleys and silent streets until at last she came to the churchyard. It was dark and lonely there, but she picked the stinging nettles and hurried back to the palace with them.

One man saw her—the chancellor, who watched while others slept. Surely now all his opinions of the queen were justified, for only a witch would gather nettles in the churchyard in the dark of the night. The next day the chancellor told the king what he had seen and what he feared. And the king, for the first time, had doubt in his heart. He pretended to sleep now at night, but no quiet sleep came to his eyes. Each night he saw how Elise got up and stole away to the little green room. Day by day his face grew darker; Elise saw it, and it added to the suffering she was already enduring for her brothers' sakes.

Still, she took heart, for now she had almost reached the end of her labors. Only one shirt of mail was wanting. But again she had no more flax; not a single nettle was left. Once more she must go to the churchyard to pluck more nettles. She thought with dread of the solitary walk and darkness, but her courage was strong and she set forth on her journey.

And the king and the chancellor followed her. They saw her disappear within the grated gateway of the churchyard. The king was filled with sorrow, for now he thought, as the chancellor did, that Elise was in truth a witch.

"The people must judge her," he said.

And the people judged. "Let her be consumed in glowing flames!" they said.

Elise was led away from her beautiful royal rooms to a dark, damp dungeon where the wind whistled through the grated window. Instead of silks and linens for her bed, they gave her the bundle of nettles for a pillow and the shirts of mail for a covering. They could not have given Elise anything more precious.

She set to work again, and towards evening she heard the rustle of swan's wings close to her window. It was her youngest brother. He had found her at last. He was filled with joy, although he knew the coming night might be her last. Still, her task was almost finished and her brothers were near.

Elise worked all the long night. The little mice ran about the floor bringing nettles to her feet, so as to give what help they could; and a thrush sat on the grating of the window and sang all night to keep up her courage.

Just before dawn her brothers reached the palace and begged to be taken to the king. This could not be done, was the answer; the king was asleep and no one dared wake him. All their entreaties and

threats were useless. The guard turned out, and even
the king himself came to see what was the matter.
But just then the sun rose, and no more brothers
were to be seen; only eleven wild swans hovered over
the palace.

All the people streamed out of the town gates to
see the witch burnt. A miserable old horse drew the
cart in which Elise sat. They had put a smock of
green sacking upon her, but all her beautiful hair
hung loose about her and covered her like a shining
mantle. Her cheeks were deathly pale, and her
fingers unceasingly twisted the green flax. Ten shirts
of mail lay completed at her feet, and she worked
away on the eleventh.

The people scoffed at her. "See how the witch
works at her sorcery," they said. "There she sits with
it in her hands instead of a prayer book. Tear it
away from her into a thousand bits!"

The crowd pressed in to destroy the shirts of mail,
but just then eleven wild swans flew down and
perched on the cart, making a ring around it with
their great wings. The people drew back in terror.

And when the executioner reached down to take
Elise out of the cart, she stood up and threw the
eleven shirts over the swans. And eleven handsome
princes stood in the cart with the queen.

"Now I may speak! I am innocent," said Elise. And

then, so great had been the strain and the terror and the suffering she had endured that she fell lifeless in her brothers' arms.

"Yes, innocent she is indeed," said the eldest brother, and he told them all that had happened.

While the prince spoke, every faggot in the pile that was to have burned Elise took root and shot out branches until a great high hedge of red roses had arisen. At the very top was one pure white blossom that shone like a star. The king broke this off and laid it on Elise's heart, and she woke with joy and peace within her.

Then all the church bells began to ring of their own accord, the fragrance of roses filled the air, singing birds flocked around, and surely such a procession went back to the palace as no king had ever seen before! The youngest prince walked in the procession by the side of the king and the queen. Elise had not quite finished his coat of mail, and for the rest of his life he had one arm and one white wild swan's wing.

NELLA'S DANCING SHOES

from *Italian Peepshow* by Eleanor Farjeon

O<small>NCE</small> upon a time there was a beautiful dancer who lived in a garden in Italy. She was called Nella.

Nella was the loveliest dancer in the world, and all the people wanted her to come and dance at their parties. In the evening she would go down to Florence to their long salons hung with blue satin embroidered with flowers, or red velvet printed with gold, and dance on the polished floors under twelve enormous chandeliers glittering with lights and lustres, which hung down like long diamond ear-drops in a Queen's ears; or else she would dance in their gardens on the lawns among the statues and roses and fountains, where all the trees were hung with lights like coloured stars. And whenever she danced in her rose-red velvet dancing slippers, all the peo-

ple clapped their hands and shouted, "*Brava,* Nella!
Brava! Brava!"

In Nella's cupboard at home were rows and rows
of other slippers, of gold, and glass, and silk, and
leather; but she never wore any of them when she
went to dance for the people. For the rose-red velvet
slippers were magic slippers which made her dance
better than anyone else in Italy; and when she wore
her other slippers, she couldn't dance at all. Nobody
knew this but Nella.

One day Nella was in her garden picking roses,
and because the dew was on the grass she had taken
off her red velvet slippers and left them by her chair.
Suddenly a great Eagle swooped out of the sky,
caught the slippers in his beak, and flew away as
swiftly as he had come. Nella gave a scream and
stood on tiptoe, and reached out her arms, trying to
touch the sky. But it was no good; the slippers and
the Eagle had vanished entirely.

Then Nella sat down and cried and cried. She
was to dance that night for the Prince of Florence,
but when the people came to fetch her she was still
sitting crying in the garden, and she wouldn't tell
them why. She only sobbed and said she wouldn't
dance. They entreated in vain—no! she wouldn't
dance. She couldn't, of course, because she had lost

her magic slippers. Every day after that she sat in the garden watching the sky, and every night the people were sad because Nella, their beautiful dancer, would dance for them no more.

One day as Nella sat watching the sky for the Eagle she saw a rush of wings overhead. It was not the Eagle, however, but a flight of Swallows.

"Oh, Swallows!" cried Nella. "You go about in the sky as people go about on earth, so have you seen the great Eagle who stole my red velvet slippers?"

But the Swallows had never seen or heard of him, and flew away, and Nella wept.

The next day as she was watching, a flock of Wild Swans flew over her head.

"Oh, Swans!" cried Nella. "You go over more places in a year than most men travel in a lifetime, so have you seen the great Eagle who stole my red velvet slippers?"

But the Swans could give her no news of him, and *they* flew away, and Nella wept.

The next day as she was watching, she saw a thousand Starlings twinkle like stars over her garden.

"Oh, Starlings!" cried Nella. "You have been everywhere among the clouds, so have you in your travels ever met the great Eagle who stole my red velvet slippers?"

But the Starlings could tell her no more than the Swans and the Swallows, and they also flew away, and Nella wept.

On the fourth day as she sat in her garden a single shadow fluttered on the grass, and looking up, she saw that it was made by a green Parrot with one red feather in his tail.

"Oh, Parrot!" cried Nella. "You live in strange countries and have seen many things, so have you seen the great Eagle who stole my red velvet slippers?"

"Certainly I have," said the Parrot.

"Oh, where?" cried Nella.

"I was sitting on a coconut-tree in a Jungle," said the Parrot, "and the Eagle flew over my head with your slippers in his beak. When he reached the very middle of the Jungle, he opened his beak and dropped the slippers, and that was the last I saw of him or them."

"Oh, Parrot!" cried Nella. "Where is the Jungle?"

"In the very middle of India," said the Parrot, and flew away.

Then Nella began to weep again, for it seemed to her that her precious slippers might as well be in the Eagle's beak as in the middle of India, for all the use they were to her.

Just then she heard a voice say, "Come, come, I wouldn't cry if I were you!" and looking up, she saw the Fan-Man looking through the gate. He was long and thin and dressed in green, and he had a green paper fan in his hand.

"What *would* you do, then?" said Nella. "The Eagle has dropped my red slippers in the very middle of the Jungle in the very middle of India, so there's nothing to do but cry. If I had wings like an Eagle or a Swallow or a Swan or a Starling or a Parrot, I wouldn't need to cry."

"Tush, tush!" said the Fan-Man. "There are more ways of flying than with wings."

Then he came into the garden and told Nella to stand on tiptoe as though she were going to dance, and when she was on the very points of her toes he opened his fan and fanned her. Up she went into the air like a bird, and after her went the Fan-Man, fanning with all his might. He fanned her right across Italy and Turkey and Persia until they reached India; and when he had fanned her to the very middle of the Jungle, the Fan-Man stopped, and Nella dropped.

Now in the very middle of the Jungle in the very middle of India there is a Blue Pool, so Nella dropped into the Pool and went down and down and down till she got to the bottom. At the bottom of the Pool she found the Blue Nymph of the Pool sitting on a lotus leaf, and to Nella's great joy the Nymph

77

had the red velvet slippers on. But as she had never seen slippers before, and hadn't the least idea what they were for, instead of having them on her feet she had hung them in her ears, where they dangled like a pair of red earrings.

Nella clasped her hands and cried, "Nymph, Nymph, give me my slippers!"

"That I won't!" said the Nymph. "They are *my* slippers, for the Eagle who brings me things brought them to me, and they are the prettiest things I ever saw."

"Then you haven't seen those I wear on my feet," said Nella, and she put out her little feet which happened that day to be shod in her golden slippers. They were much prettier than the red ones, though not nearly so wonderful.

But the Nymph didn't know that, and anyhow she had no use for slippers to dance in, but only to hang in her ears, so she eagerly asked,"Will you change?"

"If you wish it," said Nella. And she kicked off her golden slippers and put on her red ones, while the Blue Nymph hung the golden slippers in her ears, and looked more pleased with herself than before.

"Goodbye," said Nella.

"Goodbye," said the Blue Nymph.

Then Nella rose to the top of the Pool, where the Fan-Man was waiting for her. As soon as he saw her he spread his fan again, and in another moment she was sailing over India and Persia and Turkey and Italy. And when they came to her own rose garden, the Fan-Man stopped, and Nella dropped.

The first thing she did was to stand on her toes and dance.

The next thing she did was to send word to the town, saying, "Tonight I will dance for the Prince of Florence."

And that night, under thousands of stars, amongst thousands of coloured lights, Nella danced on the lawn in her red velvet slippers better than she had ever danced before, and all the people, overjoyed to have their beautiful Nella dancing for them again, climbed on the chairs and the tables, and clapped their hands, shouting:

"*Brava*, Nella! *Brava, brava!*"

GAMMELYN, THE DRESSMAKER

from *Moonshine and Clover* by Laurence Housman

THERE was once upon a time a King's daughter who was about to be given in marriage to a great prince; and when the wedding-day was yet a long way off, the whole court began to concern itself as to how the bride was to be dressed. What she should wear, and how she should wear it, was the question debated by the King and his court day and night, almost without interruption. Whatever it was to be, it must be splendid, without peer. Must it be silk, or velvet, or satin; should it be enriched with brocade, or with gems, or sewn thick with pearls?

But when they came to ask the Princess, she said, "I will have only a dress of beaten gold, light as gossamer, thin as bee's-wing, soft as swan's-down."

Then the King, calling his chief goldsmith, told

him to make for the Princess the dress of beaten gold. But the goldsmith knew no way how such a dress was to be made, and his answer to the King was, "Sire, the thing is not to be done."

Then the King grew very angry, for he said, "What a Princess can find it in her head to wish, some man must find it in his wits to accomplish." So he put the chief goldsmith in prison to think about it, and summoning all the goldsmiths in the kingdom, told them of the Princess's wish, that a dress should be made for her of beaten gold. But every one of the goldsmiths went down on his knees to the King, saying, "Sire, the thing is not to be done." Thereupon the King clapped them all into prison, promising to cut off all their heads if in three weeks' time they had not put them together to some purpose and devised a plan for making such a dress as the Princess desired.

Now just then Gammelyn was passing through the country, and when he heard of all this, he felt very sorry for the goldsmiths, who had done nothing wrong, but had told honest truth about themselves to the King. So he set his bright wits to work, and at last said, "I think I can save the goldsmiths their heads, for I have found a way of making such a dress as this fine Princess desires."

Then he went to the King and said, "I have a way for making a dress of beaten gold."

"But," said the King, "have a care, for if you fail I shall assuredly cut off your head."

All the same Gammelyn took that risk willingly and set to work. And first he asked that the Princess would tell him what style of dress it should be; and the Princess said, "Beaten gold, light as gossamer, thin as bee's-wing, soft as swan's-down, and it must be made thus." So she showed him of what fashion sleeve, and bodice, and train should be. Then Gammelyn caused to be made (for he had a palace full of workers put under him) a most lovely dress, in the fashion the Princess had named, of white cambric closely woven; and the Princess came wondering at him, saying that it was to be only of beaten gold.

"You wait a while!" said Gammelyn, for he had no liking for the Princess. Then he asked the King for gold out of his treasury; but the King supplied him instead with gold from the stores of the imprisoned goldsmiths. So he put it in a sack, and carried it to a mill, and said to the miller, "Grind me this sack full of gold into flour." At first the miller stared at him for a madman, but when he saw the letter in Gammelyn's hands which the King had written, and which said, "I'll cut off your head if you don't!" then he set to with a will and ground the gold into fine golden flour. So Gammelyn shouldered his sack and jogged back to the palace. The next thing he did was to summon all the gold-beaters in the kingdom, which he did easily enough with the King's letter; for directly they saw the words, "I'll cut off your head if you don't!" and the King's signature beneath, they came running as fast as their legs could carry them, till all the streets which led up to the palace were full of them.

Then Gammelyn chose a hundred of the strongest, and took them into the chamber where the wedding-dress was in making. And the dress he took and spread out on iron tables and, sprinkling the golden flour all over it, set the men to beat day and night for a whole week. And at the end of the week there was a splendid dress, that looked as if it were of pure gold only. But the Princess said, "My dress must be *all* gold, and no part cambric—this will not do."

"You wait!" said Gammelyn. "It is not finished yet."

Then he made a fire of sweet spices and sandalwood, jasmine, and mignonette; and into the fire he put the wonderful dress.

The Princess screamed with grief and rage; for she was in love with the dress, though she was so nice in holding him to the conditions of the decree. But Gammelyn persevered, and what happened was this: the fire burnt away all the threads of the cambric,

but was not hot enough to melt the gold; and when
all the cambric was burnt, then he drew out of the
fire a dress of beaten gold, light as gossamer, thin
as bee's-wing, soft as swan's-down, and fragrant as
a wind when it blows through a Sultan's garden.

So all the goldsmiths were set free from prison;
and the King appointed Gammelyn his chief goldsmith.

But when the Princess saw the dress, she was so
beside herself with pride and pleasure that she must
have also a dress made of pearl, light as gossamer,
thin as bee's-wing, soft as swan's-down. And the
King sent for all his jewellers and told them that
such a dress was to be made; but they all went down
on their bended knees, crying with one voice, "Sire,
the thing is not to be done." And all the good they
got for that was that they were clapped into prison
till a way for doing it should be found.

Then the King said to Gammelyn, "Since my jewellers cannot make this dress, you must do it!"

But Gammelyn said, "Sire, that is not in our bargain."

And the only answer the King had to that was,
"I'll cut off your head if you don't."

Gammelyn sighed like a sea-shell; but determin-
ing to make the best of a bad business, he set to work.

And, as before, he made a dress in the fashion the

Princess chose, of the finest weaving. He made each part separate; the two sleeves separate, the body separate, the skirt and train separate. Then, at his desire, the King commanded that all the oysters which were dredged out of the sea should be brought to him. Out of these Gammelyn selected the five finest oysters of all; each one was the size of a tea-tray. Then he put them into a large tank, and inside each shell he put one part of the dress—the weaving of which was so fine that there was plenty of room for it, as well as for the oysters. And in course of time he drew out from each shell—from one the body, from one the skirt, from one the train, from one a sleeve, from another the other sleeve. Next he fastened each part together with thread, and put the whole dress back into the tank; and into the mouth of one oyster he put the joinery of body and skirt, and into the mouth of another the joinery of skirt and train, and into the mouth of two others the joinery of the two sleeves, and the fifth oyster he ate. So the oysters did their work, laying their soft inlay over the gown, just as they laid it over the inside of their shells; and after a time Gammelyn drew forth a dress bright and gleaming, and pure mother-o'-pearl. But "No," said the Princess, "it must be all pure pearl, with nothing of thread in it."

But, "Wait a while!" said Gammelyn. "I have not finished yet."

So by a decree of the King he caused to be gathered together all the moths in the kingdom—millions of moths; and he put them all into a bare iron room along with the dress, and sealed the doors and windows with red sealing-wax. The Princess wept and sighed for the dress: "It will be all eaten," said she.

"Then I shall cut off his head," said the King. But for all that, Gammelyn persevered.

And when he opened the door they found that every thread had been eaten away by the moths, while the mother-o'-pearl had been left uninjured. So the dress was a perfect pearl, light as gossamer, thin as bee's-wing, soft as swan's-down; and the King made Gammelyn his chief jeweller, and set all the other jewellers free.

Then the Princess was so delighted that she wished to have one more dress also, made all of butterflies' wings. "That were easily done," said Gammelyn, "but it were cruel to ask for such a dress to be made."

Nevertheless the Princess would have it so, and *he* should make it. "I'll cut off your head if you don't," said the King.

Gammelyn bumbled like a bee; but all he said was, "Many million butterflies will be wanted for such a work: you must let me have again the two dresses—the pearl, and the gold—for butterflies love bright colours that gleam and shine; and with these alone can I gather them all to one place."

Gammelyn, the Dressmaker

So the Princess gave him the two dresses; and he went to the highest part of the palace, out onto the battlements of the great tower. There he faced towards the west, where lay a new moon, louting towards the setting sun; and he laid the two robes, one on either arm, spreading them abroad, till they looked like two wings—a gold and a pearl. And a beam of the sun came and kissed the gold wing, and a pale quivering thread of moonlight touched the pearl wing; and Gammelyn sang:

"Light of the moon,
  Light of the sun,
  Pearl of the sky,
  Gold from on high,
      Hearken to me!

"Light of the moon,
  Pearl of the sea,
  Gold of the land
  Here in my hand,
      I render to thee.

"Butterflies come!
  Carry us home,
  Gold of the gnome,
      Pearl of the sea."

And as he sang, out of the east came a soft muttering of wings and a deep moving mass like a bright storm-cloud. And out of the sun ran a long gold finger, and out of the moon a pale shivering finger of pearl, and touching the gold and the pearl, these became verily wings and not dresses. Then before the Princess could scream more than once, or the King say anything about cutting off heads, the bright cloud in the east became a myriad myriad of butterflies. And drawn by the falling flashing sun, and by the faint falling moon, and fanned by the million wings of his fellow-creatures, Gammelyn sprang out from the palace wall on the crest of the butterfly-wind and flew away brighter and farther each moment; and followed by his myriad train of butterflies, he passed out of sight and in that country was never heard of again.

THE PRINCESS AND THE VAGABONE

from *The Way of the Storyteller* by Ruth Sawyer

ONCE, in the golden time, when an Irish king sat in every province and plenty covered the land, there lived in Connaught a grand old king with one daughter. She was as tall and slender as the reeds that grow by Lough Erne, and her face was the fairest in seven counties. This was more the pity, for the temper she had did not match it at all, at all; it was the blackest and ugliest that ever fell to the birthlot of a princess. She was proud, she was haughty; her tongue had the length and the sharpness of the thorns on a *sidheog* bush; and from the day she was born till long after she was a woman grown she was never heard to say a kind word or known to do a kind deed to a living creature.

As each year passed, the King would think to himself: " 'Tis the New Year will see her better."

But it was worse instead of better she grew, until
one day the King found himself at the end of his
patience, and he groaned aloud as he sat alone,
drinking his poteen.

"Faith, another man shall have her for the next
eighteen years, for, by my soul, I've had my fill of
her!"

So it came about, as I am telling ye, that the King
sent word to the nobles of the neighboring provinces
that whosoever would win the consent of his daughter in marriage should have half of his kingdom and
the whole of his blessing. On the day that she was
eighteen they came: a wonderful procession of earls,
dukes, princes, and kings, riding up to the castle
gate, a-courting. The air was filled with the ring of
the silver trappings on their horses, and the courtyard was gay with the colors of their bratas and the
long cloaks they wore, riding. The King made each
welcome according to his rank; and then he sent
a serving-man to his daughter, bidding her come
and choose her suitor, the time being ripe for her
to marry. It was a courteous message that the King
sent, but the Princess heard little of it. She flew into
the hall on the heels of the serving-man, like a fowl-
hawk after a bantam cock. Her eyes burned with
the anger that was hot in her heart, while she

stamped her foot in the King's face until the rafters rang with the noise of it.

"So, ye will be giving me away for the asking— to any one of these blithering fools who has a rag to his back or a castle to his name?"

The King grew crimson at her words. He was ashamed that they should all hear how sharp was her tongue; moreover, he was fearsome lest they should take to their heels and leave him with a shrew on his hands for another eighteen years. He was hard at work piecing together a speech when the Princess strode past him on to the first suitor in the line.

"At any rate, I'll not be choosing ye, ye long-legged corn-crake," and she gave him a sound kick as she went on to the next. He was a large man with a shaggy beard; and, seeing how the first suitor had fared, he tried a wee bit of a smile on her while his hand went out coaxingly. She saw, and the anger in her grew threefold. She sprang at him, digging the two of her hands deep in his beard, and then she wagged his foolish head back and forth, screaming: "Take that, and that, and that, ye old whiskered rascal!"

It was a miracle that any beard was left on his face the way that she pulled it. But she let him go

free at last, and turned to a thin, sharp-faced prince
with a monstrous long nose. The nose took her fancy,
and she gave it a tweak, telling the prince to take
himself home before he did any damage with it. The
next one she called "pudding-face" and slapped his
fat cheeks until they were purple, and the poor lad
groaned with the sting of it.

"Go back to your trough, for I'll not marry a
grunter, i' faith," said she.

She moved swiftly down the line in less time than
it takes for the telling. It came to the mind of many
of the suitors that they would be doing a wise thing
if they betook themselves off before their turn came;
as many of them as were not fastened to the floor
with fear started away. There happened to be a fat,
crooked-legged prince from Leinster just making for
the door when the Princess looked around. In a trice
she reached out for the tongs that stood on the
hearth near by, and she laid it across his shoulders,
sending him spinning into the yard.

"Take that, ye old gander, and good riddance to
ye!" she cried after him.

It was then that she saw looking at her a great
towering giant of a man; and his eyes burned
through hers, deep down into her soul. So great was
he that he could have picked her up with a single

94

hand and thrown her after the gander; and she knew it and yet she felt no fear. He was as handsome as Nuada of the Silver Hand; and not a mortal fault could she have found with him, not if she had tried for a hundred years. The two of them stood facing each other, flaring, as if each would spring at the other's throat the next moment; but all the while the Princess was thinking, and thinking how wonderful he was, from the top of his curling black hair, down the seven feet of him, to the golden clasps on his shoes.

What the man was thinking I cannot be telling. Like a breath of wind on smoldering turf, her liking for him set her anger fierce-burning again. She gave him a sound cuff on the ear, then turned, and with a sob in her throat she went flying from the room, the serving-men scattering before her as if she had been a hundred million robbers on a raid.

And the King? Faith, he was dumb with rage. But when he saw the blow that his daughter had given to the finest gentleman in all of Ireland, he went after her as if he had been two hundred million constables on the trail of robbers.

"Ye are a disgrace and a shame to me," said he, catching up with her and holding firmly to her two hands; "and, what's more, ye are a disgrace and a blemish to my castle and my kingdom; I'll not keep ye in it a day longer. The first traveling vagabone who comes begging at the door shall have ye for his wife."

"Will he?" and the Princess tossed her head in the King's face and went to her chamber.

The next morning a poor singing *sthronshuch* came to the castle to sell a song for a penny or a morsel of bread. The song was sweet that he sang, and the Princess listened as Oona, the tirewoman, was winding strands of her long black hair with golden thread.

"The gay young wren sang over the moor.
   'I'll build me a nest,' sang he.
' 'Twill have a thatch and a wee latched door,
   For the wind blows cold from the sea.
And I'll let no one but my true love in,
   For she is the mate for me,'
     Sang the gay young wren.

"The wee brown wren by the hedgerow cried,
   'I'll wait for him here,' cried she.
'For the way is far and the world is wide,
   And he might miss the way to me.
Long is the time when the heart is shut,
   But I'll open to none save he,'
     Sang the wee brown wren."

A strange throb came to the heart of the Princess when the song was done. She pulled her hair free from the hands of the tirewoman.

"Get silver," she said; "I would throw it to him." And when she saw the wonderment grow in Oona's face, she added: "The song pleased me. Can I not pay for what I like without having ye look at me as if ye feared my wits had flown? Go, get the silver!" But when she pushed open the grating and leaned far out to throw it, the *sthronshuch* had gone.

For the King had heard the song as well as the Princess. His rage was still with him, and when he saw who it was, he lost no time, but called him quickly inside.

"Ye are as fine a vagabone as I could wish for," he said. "Maybe ye are not knowing it, but ye are a bridegroom this day." And the King went on to tell him the whole tale. The tale being finished, he sent ten strong men to bring the Princess down.

A king's word was law in those days. The vagabone knew this; and, what's more, he knew he must marry the Princess, whether he liked it or no. The vagabone had great height, but he stooped so that it shortened the length of him. His hair was long, and it fell, uncombed and matted, about his shoulders. His brogues were patched, his hose were sadly worn, and with his rags he was the sorriest cut of a man that a maid ever laid her two eyes on. When the Princess came, she was dressed in a gown of gold, with jewels hanging from every thread of it, and her cap was caught with a jeweled brooch. She looked as beautiful as a May morning—with a thunder-cloud rising back of the hills; and the vagabone held his breath for a moment, watching her. Then he pulled the King gently by the arm.

"I'll not have a wife that looks grander than myself. If I marry your daughter, I must marry her in rags—the same as my own."

The King agreed 'twas a good idea, and sent for the worst dress of rags in the whole countryside. The rags were fetched, the Princess dressed, the priest brought, and the two of them married; and, though she cried and she kicked and she cuffed and she prayed, she was the vagabone's wife—hard and fast.

"Now take her, and good luck go with ye," said the King. Then his eyes fell on the tongs by the hearth. "Here, take these along—they may come in handy on the road."

Out of the castle gate, across the gardens, and into the country that lay beyond went the Princess and the vagabone. The sky was blue over their heads and the air was full of spring; each wee creature that passed them on the road seemed bursting with the

joy of it. There was naught but anger in the Princess's heart, however; and what was in the heart of the vagabone I cannot be telling. This I know, that he sang the "Song of the Wren" as they went. Often and often the Princess turned back on the road or sat down, swearing she would go no farther; and often and often did she feel the weight of the tongs across her shoulders that day.

At noon the two sat down by the crossroads to rest.

"I am hungry," said the Princess; "not a morsel of food have I tasted this day. Ye will go get me some."

"Not I, my dear," said the vagabone; "ye will go beg for yourself."

"Never," said the Princess.

"Then ye'll go hungry," said the vagabone; and that was all. He lighted his pipe and went to sleep with one eye open and the tongs under him.

One, two, three hours passed, and the sun hung low in the sky. The Princess sat there until hunger drove her to her feet. She rose wearily and stumbled to the road. It might have been the sound of wheels that had started her, I cannot be telling; but as she reached the road a great coach drawn by six black horses came galloping up. The Princess made a sign for it to stop; though she was in rags, yet she was still so beautiful that the coachman drew in the horses and asked her what she was wanting.

"I am near to starving," and as she spoke the tears started to her eyes, while a new soft note crept into her voice. "Do ye think your master could spare me a bit of food—or a shilling?" and the hand that had been used to strike went out for the first time to beg.

It was a prince who rode inside the coach that day, and he heard her. Reaching out a fine, big hamper through the window, he told her she was hearty welcome to whatever she found in it, along with his blessing. But as she put up her arms for it, just, she looked—and saw that the prince was none other than the fat suitor whose face she had slapped on the day before. Then anger came back to her again, for the shame of begging from him. She emptied the hamper—chicken pasty, jam, currant bread, and all—on top of his head, peering through the window, and threw the empty basket at the coachman. Away drove the coach; away ran the Princess, and threw herself, sobbing, on the ground near the vagabone.

" 'Twas a good dinner that ye lost," said the vagabone; and that was all.

That night they reached a wee scrap of a cabin

on the side of a hill. The vagabone climbed the steps and opened the door. "Here we are at home, my dear," said he.

"What kind of a home do ye call this?" and the Princess stamped her foot. "Faith, I'll not live in it."

"Then ye can live outside; it's all the same to me." The vagabone went in and closed the door after him; and in a moment he was whistling merrily the song of the wee brown wren.

The Princess sat down on the ground and nursed her poor tired knees. She had walked many a mile that day, with a heavy heart and an empty stomach —two of the worst traveling companions ye can find. The night came down, black as a raven's wing; the dew fell, heavy as rain, wetting the rags and chilling the Princess to the marrow. The wind blew fresh from the sea, and the wolves began their howling in the woods near by; and at last, what with the cold and the fear and the loneliness of it, she could bear it no longer, and she crept softly up to the cabin and went in.

"There's the creepy-stool by the fire, waiting for ye," said the vagabone; and that was all. But late in the night he lifted her from the chimney corner where she had dropped asleep and laid her gently on the bed, which was freshly made and clean. And he sat by the hearth till dawn, keeping the turf piled high on the fire, so that cold would not waken her. Once he left the hearth; coming to the bedside, he stood a moment to watch her while she slept, and he stooped and kissed the wee pink palm of her hand that lay there like a half-closed lough lily.

Next morning the first thing the Princess asked was where was the breakfast, and where were the servants to wait on her, and where were some decent clothes.

"Your servants are your own two hands, and they will serve ye well when ye teach them how," was the answer she got.

"I'll have neither breakfast nor clothes if I have to be getting them myself. And shame on ye for treating a wife so," and the Princess caught up a piggin and threw it at the vagabone.

He jumped clear of it, and it struck the wall behind him. "Have your own way, my dear," and he left her, to go out on the bogs and cut turf.

That night the Princess hung the kettle and made stir-about and griddle bread for the two of them.

" 'Tis the best I have tasted since I was a lad and my mother made the baking," said the vagabone, and that was all. But often and often his lips touched the braids of her hair as she passed him in the dark; and again he sat through the night, keeping the fire and mending her wee leather brogues, that they might be whole against the morrow.

Next day he brought some sally twigs and showed her how to weave them into creels to sell on coming market-day. But the twigs cut her fingers until they bled, and the Princess cried, making the vagabone white with rage. Never had she seen such a rage in another creature. He threw the sally twigs about the cabin, making them whirl and eddy like leaves before an autumn wind; he stamped upon the half-made creel, crushing it to pulp under his feet; and, catching up the table, he tore it to splinters, throwing the fragments into the fire, where they blazed.

"By Saint Patrick, 'tis a bad bargain that ye are! I will take ye this day to the castle in the next county, where I hear they are needing a scullery-maid; and there I'll apprentice ye to the King's cook."

"I will not go," said the Princess; but even as she spoke fear showed in her eyes and her knees began shaking in under her.

"Aye, but ye will, my dear," and the vagabone took up the tongs quietly from the hearth.

For a month the Princess worked in the castle of the King, and all that time she never saw the vagabone. Often and often she said to herself, fiercely, that she was well rid of him; but often, as she sat alone after her work in the cool of the night, she would wish for the song of the wee brown wren, while a new loneliness crept deeper and deeper into her heart.

She worked hard about the kitchen, and as she scrubbed the pots and turned the spit and cleaned the floor with fresh white sand, she listened to the wonderful tales the other servants had to tell of the King. They had it that he was the handsomest, aye, and the strongest, king in all of Ireland: and every man and child and little creature in his kingdom worshiped him. And after the tales were told the Princess would say to herself: "If I had not been so proud and free with my tongue, I might have married such a king, and ruled his kingdom with him, learning kindness."

Now it happened one day that the Princess was told to be unusually spry and careful about her work; and there was a monstrous deal of it to be done: cakes to be iced and puddings to be boiled, fat ducks to be roasted, and a whole suckling pig put on the spit to turn.

"What's the meaning of all this?" asked the Princess.

"Ochone, ye poor feeble-minded girl!" and the cook looked at her pityingly. "Haven't ye heard the King is to be married this day to the fairest princess in seven counties?"

"Once that was I," thought the Princess, and she sighed.

"What makes ye sigh?" asked the cook.

"I was wishing, just, that I could be having a peep at her and the King."

"Faith, that's possible. Do your work well, and maybe I can put ye where ye can see without being seen."

So it came about, as I am telling ye, at the end of the day, when the feast was ready and the guests come, that the Princess was hidden behind the broidered curtains in the great hall. There, where no one could see her, she watched the hundreds upon hundreds of fair ladies and fine noblemen in their silken dresses and shining coats, all silver and gold, march back and forth across the hall, laughing and talking and making merry among themselves. Then the pipers began to play, and everybody was still. From the farthest end of the hall came two and twenty lads in white and gold; and these were followed by two and twenty pipers in green and gold and two and twenty bowmen in saffron and gold, and, last of all, the King.

A scream, a wee wisp of a cry, broke from the Princess, and she would have fallen had she not caught one of the curtains. For the King was as tall and strong and beautiful as Nuada of the Silver Hand;

and from the top of his curling black hair, down the seven feet of him, to the golden clasps of his shoes he was every whit as handsome as he had been that day when she had cuffed him in her father's castle.

The King heard the cry and stopped the pipers. "I think," said he, "there's a scullery-maid behind the curtains. Someone fetch her to me."

A hundred hands pulled the Princess out; a hundred more pushed her across the hall to the feet of the King, and held her there, fearing lest she escape. "What were ye doing there?" the King asked.

"Looking at ye, and wishing I had the undoing of things I have done," and the Princess hung her head and sobbed piteously.

"Nay, sweetheart, things are best as they are," and there came a look into the King's eyes that blinded those watching, so that they turned away and left the two alone.

"Heart of mine," he went on, softly, "are ye not knowing me?"

"Ye are putting more shame on me because of my evil tongue and the blow my hand gave ye that day."

"I' faith, it is not so. Look at me."

Slowly the eyes of the Princess looked into the eyes of the King. For a moment she could not be reading them; she was as a child who pores over a strange tale after the light fades and it has grown too dark to see. But bit by bit the meaning of it came to her, and her heart grew glad with the wonder of it. Out went her arms to him with the cry of loneliness that had been hers so long.

"I never dreamed that it was ye, never once."

"Can ye ever love and forgive?" asked the King.

"Hush ye!" and the Princess laid her finger on his lips.

The tirewomen were called and she was led away. Her rags were changed for a dress that was spun from gold and woven with pearls, and her beauty shone about her like a great light. They were married again that night, for none of the guests were knowing of the first wedding long ago.

Late o' that night a singing *sthronshuch* came under the Princess's window, and very softly the words of his song came to her:

"The gay young wren sang over the moor.
　'I'll build me a nest,' sang he.
'Twill have a thatch and a wee latched door,
　For the wind blows cold from the sea.
And I'll let no one but my true love in,
　For she is the mate for me,'
　　Sang the gay young wren.

"The wee brown wren by the hedgerow cried,
　'I'll wait for him here,' cried she.

'For the way is far and the world is wide,
And he might miss the way to me.
Long is the time when the heart is shut,
But I'll open to none save he,'
Sang the wee brown wren."

The grating opened slowly; the Princess leaned far out, her eyes like stars in the night, and when she spoke there was naught but gentleness and love in her voice.

"Here is the silver I would have thrown ye on a day long gone by. Shall I throw it now, or will ye come for it?"

And that was how a princess of Connaught was won by a king who was a vagabone.

KATCHA AND THE DEVIL

from *The Shepherd's Nosegay,* retold by Parker
Fillmore and edited by Katherine Love

HERE was once a woman named Katcha
who lived in a village where she owned her own
cottage and garden. She had money besides, but
little good it did her because she was such an ill-
tempered vixen that nobody, not even the poorest
laborer, would marry her. Nobody would even work
for her, no matter what she paid, for she couldn't
open her mouth without scolding, and whenever she
scolded, she raised her shrill voice until you could
hear it a mile away. The older she grew, the worse
she became, until by the time she was forty, she
was as sour as vinegar.

Now as it always happens in a village, every Sunday afternoon there was a dance either at the burgo-
master's or at the tavern. As soon as the bagpipes
sounded, the boys all crowded into the room and

the girls gathered outside and looked in the windows. Katcha was always the first at the window. The music would strike up and the boys would beckon the girls to come in and dance, but no one ever beckoned Katcha. Even when she paid the piper, no one ever asked her to dance. Yet she came Sunday after Sunday just the same.

One Sunday afternoon as she was hurrying to the tavern, she thought to herself: "Here I am getting old and yet I've never once danced with a boy! Plague take it, today I'd dance with the devil if he asked me!"

She was in a fine rage by the time she reached the tavern, where she sat down near the stove and looked around to see what girls the boys had invited to dance.

Suddenly a stranger in hunter's green came in. He sat down at a table near Katcha and ordered drink. When the serving maid brought the beer, he reached over to Katcha and asked her to drink with him. At first she was much taken back at this attention, then she pursed her lips coyly and pretended to refuse, but finally she accepted.

When they had finished drinking, he pulled a ducat from his pocket, tossed it to the piper, and called out:

"Clear the floor, boys! This is for Katcha and me alone!"

The boys snickered and the girls giggled, hiding behind each other and stuffing their aprons into their mouths so that Katcha wouldn't hear them laughing. But Katcha wasn't noticing them at all. Katcha was dancing with a fine young man! If the whole world had been laughing at her, Katcha wouldn't have cared.

The stranger danced with Katcha all afternoon and all evening. Not once did he dance with anyone else. He bought her marzipan and sweet drinks, and when the hour came to go home, he escorted her through the village.

"Ah," sighed Katcha when they reached her cottage and it was time to part, "I wish I could dance with you forever!"

"Very well," said the stranger. "Come with me."

"Where do you live?"

"Put your arm around my neck and I'll tell you."

Katcha put both arms about his neck, and instantly the man changed into a devil and flew straight down to hell.

At the gates of hell he stopped and knocked.

His comrades came and opened the gates, and when they saw that he was exhausted, they tried to take Katcha off his neck. But Katcha held on tight, and nothing they could do or say would make her budge.

The devil finally had to appear before the Prince of Darkness himself with Katcha still glued to his neck.

"What's that thing you've got around your neck?" the Prince asked.

So, the devil told how, as he was walking about on earth, he had heard Katcha say she would dance with the devil himself if he asked her. "So I asked her to dance with me," the devil said. "Afterwards just to frighten her a little, I brought her down to hell. And now she won't let go of me!"

"Serves you right, you dunce!" the Prince said. "How often have I told you to use common sense when you go wandering around on earth! You might have known Katcha would never let go of a man once she had him!"

"I beg Your Majesty to make her let go!" the poor devil implored.

"I will not!" said the Prince. "You'll have to carry her back to earth yourself and get rid of her as best you can. Perhaps this will be a lesson to you."

So, the devil, very tired and very cross, shambled back to earth with Katcha still clinging to his neck. He tried every way to get her off. He promised her wooded hills and rich meadows if she would but let him go. He cajoled her, he cursed her, but all to no avail. Katcha still held on.

Breathless and discouraged, he came at last to a meadow where a shepherd, wrapped in a great shaggy sheepskin coat, was tending his flocks. The devil transformed himself into an ordinary-looking man so that the shepherd didn't recognize him.

"Hi, there," the shepherd said, "what's that you're carrying?"

"Don't ask me," the devil said with a sigh. "I'm so worn out I'm nearly dead. I was walking yonder not thinking of anything at all when along comes a woman and jumps on my back and won't let go. I'm trying to carry her to the nearest village to get rid of her there, but I don't believe I'm able. My legs are giving out."

The shepherd, who was a good-natured chap, said: "I tell you what. I'll help you. I can't leave my sheep long, but I'll carry her halfway."

"Oh," said the devil, "I'd be very grateful if you did!"

So, the shepherd yelled at Katcha: "Hi, there, you! Catch hold of me!"

When Katcha saw that the shepherd was a handsome youth, she let go of the devil and leapt upon the shepherd's back, catching hold of the collar of his sheepskin coat.

Now the young shepherd soon found that the long shaggy coat and Katcha made a pretty heavy load

115

for walking. In a few moments he was sick of his bargain and began casting about for some way of getting rid of Katcha.

Presently he came to a pond, and he thought to himself that he'd like to throw her in. He wondered how he could do it. Perhaps he could manage it by throwing his greatcoat with her. The coat was so loose that he thought he could slip out of it without Katcha's discovering what he was doing. Very cautiously he slipped out one arm. Katcha didn't move. He slipped out the other arm. Still Katcha didn't move. He unlooped the first button. Still Katcha noticed nothing. He unlooped the second button and kerplunk! he had pitched coat and Katcha and all into the middle of the pond!

When he got back to his sheep, the devil looked at him in amazement.

"Where's Katcha?" he gasped.

"Oh," the shepherd said, pointing over his shoulder with his thumb, "I decided to leave her up yonder in a pond."

"My dear friend," the devil cried, "I thank you! You have done me a great favor. If it hadn't been for you, I might be carrying Katcha till doomsday. I'll never forget you and sometime I'll reward you. As you don't know who it is you've helped, I must tell you I'm a devil."

With these words the devil vanished.

For a moment the shepherd was dazed. Then he laughed and said to himself: "Well, if they're all as stupid as he is, we ought to be able for them!"

The country where the shepherd lived was ruled over by a dissolute young duke who passed his days in riotous living and his nights in carousing. He gave over the affairs of state to two governors who were as bad as he. With extortionate taxes and unjust fines they robbed the people until the whole land was crying out against them.

Now one day for amusement the duke summoned an astrologer to court and ordered him to read in the planets the fate of himself and his two governors. When the astrologer had cast a horoscope for each of the three reprobates, he was greatly disturbed and tried to dissuade the duke from questioning him further.

"Such danger," he said, "threatens your life and the lives of your two governors that I fear to speak."

"Whatever it is," said the duke, "speak. But I warn you to speak the truth, for if what you say does not come to pass, you will forfeit your life."

The astrologer bowed and said: "Hear then, oh Duke, what the planets foretell. Before the second quarter of the moon, on such and such a day, at such and such an hour, a devil will come and carry off

the two governors. At the full of the moon on such
and such a day, at such and such an hour, the same
devil will come for Your Highness and carry you off
to hell."

The duke pretended to be unconcerned, but in
his heart he was deeply shaken. The voice of the
astrologer sounded to him like the voice of judgment,
and for the first time conscience began to trouble
him.

As for the governors, they couldn't eat a bite of
food and were carried from the palace half-dead
with fright. They piled their ill-gotten wealth into
wagons and rode away to their castles, where they
barred all the doors and windows in order to keep
the devil out.

The duke reformed. He gave up his evil ways and
corrected the abuses of state in the hope of averting
if possible his cruel fate.

The poor shepherd had no inkling of any of these
things. He tended his flocks from day to day and
never bothered his head about the happenings in the
great world.

Suddenly one day the devil appeared before him
and said: "I have come, my friend, to repay you for
your kindness. When the moon is in its first quarter,
I was to carry off the former governors of this land

because they robbed the poor and gave the duke
evil counsel. However, they're behaving themselves
now, so they're to be given another chance. But they
don't know this. Now on such and such a day do
you go to the first castle where a crowd of people
will be assembled. When a cry goes up and the gates
open and I come dragging out the governor, do you
step up to me and say: 'What do you mean by this?
Get out of here or there'll be trouble!' I'll pretend to
be greatly frightened and make off. Then ask the
governor to pay you two bags of gold, and if he
haggles, just threaten to call me back. After that go
on to the castle of the second governor and do the
same thing and demand the same pay. I warn you,
though, be prudent with the money and use it only
for good. When the moon is full, I'm to carry off the
duke himself, for he was so wicked that he's to have
no second chance. So, don't try to save him, for if
you do, you'll pay for it with your own skin. Don't
forget!"

The shepherd remembered carefully everything
the devil told him. When the moon was in its first
quarter, he went to the first castle. A great crowd of
people was gathered outside waiting to see the devil
carry away the governor.

Suddenly there was a loud cry of despair, the gates

of the castle opened, and there was the devil, as black as night, dragging out the governor. He, poor man, was half-dead with fright.

The shepherd elbowed his way through the crowd, took the governor by the hand, and pushed the devil roughly aside.

"What do you mean by this?" he shouted. "Get out of here or there'll be trouble!"

Instantly the devil fled, and the governor fell on his knees before the shepherd and kissed his hands and begged him to state what he wanted in reward. When the shepherd asked for two bags of gold, the governor ordered that they be given him without delay.

Then the shepherd went to the castle of the second governor and went through exactly the same performance.

It goes without saying that the duke soon heard of the shepherd, for he had been anxiously awaiting the fate of the two governors. At once he sent a wagon with four horses to fetch the shepherd to the palace, and when the shepherd arrived, he begged him piteously to rescue him likewise from the devil's clutches.

"Master," the shepherd answered, "I cannot promise you anything. I have to consider my own safety. You have been a great sinner, but if you really want to reform, if you really want to rule your people justly and kindly and wisely as becomes a true ruler, then indeed I will help you even if I have to suffer hellfire in your place."

The duke declared that with God's help he would mend his ways, and the shepherd promised to come back on the fatal day.

With grief and dread the whole country awaited the coming of the full moon. In the first place the people had greeted the astrologer's prophecy with joy, but since the duke had reformed, their feelings for him had changed.

Time sped fast as time does whether joy be coming or sorrow, and all too soon the fatal day arrived.

Dressed in black and pale with fright, the duke sat expecting the arrival of the devil.

Suddenly the door flew open and the devil, black as night, stood before him. He paused a moment and then he said politely:

"Your time has come, Lord Duke, and I am here to get you!"

Without a word the duke arose and followed the devil to the courtyard, which was filled with a great multitude of people.

At that moment the shepherd, all out of breath, came pushing his way through the crowd and ran straight at the devil, shouting out:

"What do you mean by this? Get out of here or there'll be trouble!"

"What do *you* mean?" whispered the devil. "Don't you remember what I told you?"

"Hush!" the shepherd whispered back. "I don't care anything about the duke. This is to warn you! You know Katcha? She's alive and she's looking for you!"

The instant the devil heard the name of Katcha be turned and fled.

All the people cheered the shepherd, while the shepherd himself laughed in his sleeve to think that he had taken in the devil so easily.

As for the duke, he was so grateful to the shepherd that he made him his chief counselor and loved him as a brother. And well he might, for the shepherd was a sensible man and always gave him sound advice.

WHITEBEAR WHITTINGTON

from *Grandfather Tales* by Richard Chase

NE time there was a man had three daughters. His wife was dead, and the three girls they kept house for him. And one day he was fixin' to go to town, so he called his girls, asked 'em what did they want him to bring 'em. The eldest told him, says, "I want a silk dress the color of every bird in the sky."

The second girl said, "I want you to bring me a silk dress made out of every color in a rainbow."

The youngest 'un she didn't say anything. So directly he went and asked her didn't she want him to bring her something too. She studied a minute, says, "All I want is some white roses. If you see a white rosebush anywhere you might break me a basketful."

Well, he took him a basket of eggs and got on his horse and went on to town. Got all his tradin' done and started back. Rode on, rode on, come to where there was a thick wilderness of a place, saw a big rosebush 'side the road, full of white roses. So he got off his horse and broke off a few. Thought he heard something behind him, says:

"You break them
and I'll break you!"

So he stopped, looked around, waited awhile and tried to see what it was spoke, didn't see anybody nor hear it again, so he broke off some more. Then he heard it real plain—sounded like it was back in the wilderness—

"You break them
and I'll break you!"

He started to quit that time, but he still couldn't see anybody or anything, and the prettiest roses were still on the bush, so he reached out his hand to break them off—and that thing said:

"Give me what meets you
first at the gate,
you can break all you want
till your basket is full."

He thought a minute or two—and he knew that his old dog always came lopin' out in the road whenever he got in home. The old hound wasn't much good anyway—so he answered, says:

"Whatever meets me
first at the gate,
you can come take it
whenever you want."

Went ahead and broke white rosebuds till his basket was full. Got on his horse and rode on in home.

He kept lookin' for his dog to come out but the old hound was up under the house asleep and before he could whistle for it here came his youngest girl flyin' out the gate to meet him.

He hollered to her and motioned her to go back but she wasn't payin' him any mind, came right on. She took his basket and was a-carryin' on over how pretty the roses were. So she thanked him and went to helpin' him unload his saddlebags, and when they got to the house she saw he was lookin' troubled, says, "What's the matter, Daddy?" But he wouldn't tell her.

And he never came to the table when they called him to supper, just sat there on the porch lookin' back down the holler. So the girls they ate their supper, and it got dark directly and they lit the lamp. Sat there sewin' and talkin', and all at once they heard a voice out in the road—

The Blue Rose

"Send out my pay!"

Their daddy came in the house then, and told 'em what'n-all he had heard when he broke the roses. The oldest girl she said to him, says, "Aw, just send out the dog. How could it know what met you first?"

So they called the dog and sicked him out toward the gate. He ran out barkin' and then they heard him come back a-howlin', scared to death, and he crawled way back under the floor and stayed there. Then they heard it again—

"Send out my pay!"

So the two oldest girls said they wasn't afraid, said they'd go see what it was. Out they went, and directly there was a commotion at the gate and the two girls came tearin' back to the house so scared they couldn't speak. Then it hollered louder—

"Send out my pay!"

Then the youngest girl said, "I'll have to go, Daddy, but don't you worry; I'll come back some way or other."

So she gathered her up a few things in a budget and kissed her father and went on out to the gate. There stood a big white bear.

"Get up on my back," it told her. So she crawled up on its back and it started off.

The girl was cryin' so hard her nose bled and three drops of blood fell on the white bear's back. They went on, went on, and 'way up in the night she made out how they went past a big white rose-bush out in a thick wilderness. Came to a fine house out there and the white bear stopped, told her, "Get off now."

So she got off and went on in the house. The white bear came in behind her, says, "Light that lamp there on the table." So she lit the lamp, and when she turned back around there stood a good-lookin' young man. The minute she looked at him she thought the world of him. He said to her then, says, "This house and everything in it belongs to you now, and there's nothing here to hurt you."

Then he took the lamp and they went through all the rooms lookin' at all the fine things, and directly they came to a pretty bedroom and he told her, says, "Now I got a spell on me and I can't be a man but part of the time. From now on I can be a man of a night and stay with you here and be a bear of a day, or I can be a bear of a night and sleep under your bed and be a man of a day. Which had you rather I'd be?"

So she thought about it and she didn't like the idea of a bear layin' under her bed of a night so she told him she'd rather he'd be a man of a night. So that was the way it was. He was a bear in the daytime and he'd lie around outside while she kept house, and when dark came he'd be a man. He kept plenty of wood and water in the house and they'd talk together and he was good company.

So they kept on and she lived happy even if her husband did have to be a bear half the time. He told her how it was he'd been witched, said he'd get out of it some day but he didn't know just how it would be. And after three or four years she had three little babes, two boys and a girl. Then when her least one was big enough to walk she told her husband she wanted to go back to see her father again. It looked like that troubled him but he told her all right, they would go; but he said she would have to promise him not to tell *any*body anything about him, and *never* to speak his name.

"If you speak my name to any living soul I'll have to go away. And you will see me going off up the mountain and it will be awful hard for us ever to get together again."

So she promised him and early the next mornin' he took her and the three children on his back, and he let them off at her father's gate and she took her babes and went on to the house.

They were all proud to see her again and told her how pretty her children were and commenced

askin' her who her husband was and where they lived and all. She told 'em she couldn't tell. Well, they kept on at her and she kept tellin' 'em she couldn't possibly tell, so her sisters they started actin' mad and wouldn't speak to her. Still she wouldn't tell; but the next day her daddy took her aside and spoke to her about it, says, "Just tell me his name."

She thought surely she ought to tell her own father what her man's name was, so she whispered it to him—

"Whitebear Whittington."

And she hadn't but spoke it when she looked up and saw her husband and he was in the shape of a man, and he was goin' off up the Piney Mountain, and on the back of his white shirt were three drops of blood.

Well, she loved him; so she left the children there with her father and started out to try and find her man again. She took out the way he went over the Piney Mountain but she never did see him on ahead of her. But she went on and went on. Sometimes she'd think she was lost but a white bird would fly over and drop a white feather with a red speck on it, so she'd go on the way that bird was headed. Then she'd stop at a house to stay the night and they'd tell her about the fine young man had stayed there the night before, had three drops of blood on his shirt.

So she went on, went on, for seven years and that bird would fly over whenever she got down-hearted, so she didn't give up. Then late one evening she stopped at a house and called to stay the night and an old, old woman awful stricken in age came to the door, looked like she was over a hundred years old and she was walkin' on two sticks, told her to come on in. The old woman looked at her, says, "Girl, you're in bad trouble, now ain't ye?"

So she told the old lady about what'n-all had happened, and how she'd been tryin' to find her man again; and directly the old woman told her, says, "You just stay here with me now, and get rested up a little, and it may be I can help you. I got a lot of wool to work and I need somebody. Will you stay and help me about my wool?"

She said yes, she would. So the next day they got all the fleeces out and she helped pick out the burs and trash, and washed the wool in the creek, while the old woman carded. Carded so fast the girl had a time keepin' up with her and they got it all done by sundown. And that night the old woman gave her a gold chinquapin. The next day the girl she helped with the spinnin': handed the rolls of carded wool to the old lady, and it was a sight in the world

how she could spin. They got it all spun up about
dark, and that night the old woman handed her a
gold hickory nut. Then the third day the old woman
sat down at her loom and the girl kept fixin' the
bobbins and handin' 'em to her and the old loom
went *click! wham! click! wham!* all day long, and
just 'fore dark the weavin' was all done. So that
night the old woman gave her a gold walnut, says,
"Now you keep these three gold nuts and don't you
crack 'em till you're in the most trouble you could
ever be in. And if the first one don't get ye out,
crack the next, and if you have to crack the last 'un
you surely ought to be out of your trouble by then."

So she thanked the old lady and the next mornin'
she left with the three gold nuts in her apron pocket.
She went on, went on, and in three days she came
to a river and she went along the river till she came
to a washin' place where a great crowd of young
women was gathered, and there in the middle of
all them women she saw her husband. She got
through the crowd and went up to him but when he
looked at her it was just as if he never had known
her before in all his life.

He didn't have any shirt on and she saw the
women lined up before the washin' place and one
girl was down on her knees washin' his shirt with
all her might. She listened and heard 'em talkin'
about how that young man had said he'd marry the

one could wash the blood out of his shirt. So she
got in the line and fin'lly got down to the washin'
place. The one ahead of her was a big stout woman
and she was down on her knees a'washin' that shirt
so hard it looked like she'd tear it apart. Soap it and
maul it with the battlin' stick and rinse it and soap
it and maul it again, but the blood just got darker
and darker. So directly the girl said she'd like to
have her turn. That other woman didn't get up off
her knees, looked at her, says, "Humph! If I can't
get this blood out I know a puny thing like you can't
do it."

Well, that girl she just leaned down and took hold
on his shirt and gave it one rub and it was white as
snow. But before she could turn around the other
woman grabbed it and ran with it, says, "Look!
Look! I washed it out!"

So the young man he had to go home with her.

His real wife knew now that she was in the most
trouble she could ever be in. So she followed 'em
and saw what house it was, and about dark she went
there, went right in the door and cracked her gold
chinquapin. It coiled out the finest gold wool you
ever saw—just one long carded roll ready to be spun.
So she started pullin' out the gold wool and pretty
soon that other woman came in and saw it, says,
"Oh, I must have that! What will you take for it?"

"Why, I couldn't part with my gold nut."

"You name any price you want now, and I'll give it to ye."

"Let me stay this night with your man and you can have it."

"Well! I must have that gold chinquapin. You go on out and wait till I call ye."

So she took the gold chinquapin and put it away. Then she put a sleepy pillow on the young man's bed and just before he went to go to bed she gave him a sleepy dram, and then she called that girl, and when she went in to him he was sound asleep. She sat down beside him and tried to wake him up but he slept right on. So she stayed there by him all night cryin' and singin':

> "Three drops of blood I've shed for thee!
> Three little babes I've born for thee!
> Whitebear Whittington! Turn to me!"

And when daylight came that other woman made her leave. Well, the girl came back that next evening and broke the gold hickory nut. A fine spinning wheel came out of it, stood right up in the floor and started spinnin'. All you had to do was put the gold chinquapin in a crack in the logs and set the end of the wool on the spindle, and it spun right on—spin and wind, spin and wind all by itself. Hit was the finest gold thread you ever saw. And when that woman came in and saw it, said she just had to have the wheel. So the girl let her have it for another night with her man. But when she went to him he slept right on through the night because that sleepy pillow was still under his head and that woman had gone and given him another sleepy dram. So all night his wife stayed by him tryin' to wake him up—

"Three drops of blood I've shed for thee!
Three little babes I've born for thee!
Whitebear Whittington! Turn to me!"

And early in the morning that other woman came, said, "Get on out now. Your time is up."

Well, the next evening the father of that woman called the young man just before bedtime. Said he wanted to have a word with him. So they walked out a ways and the old man said to him, says, "I couldn't sleep a bit the last two nights. There's some kind of a cryin' noise been goin' on in your room, and somebody singin' a mournful song right on up through the night."

The young man said he had slept uncommon sound the last two nights, hadn't heard a thing.

"Well now," says the old man, "I want you to be sure to stay awake tonight, and listen and see what all that carryin' on is."

So that night the girl came and cracked the gold

walnut and a big loom came out of it—just r'ared up in the house time she broke the nut. It was warped with gold warp and all you had to do was feed it bobbins of that gold thread and it wove right on— all by itself. The woman she heard it a-beatin' and she came running.

"Oh, my! I must have that! What'll you take for your loom?"

The girl told her.

"Well!" she says, real hateful-like, "you can stay with him tonight but I'll tell ye right now it's the last time."

So she made the girl go out and then she looked about that sleepy pillow bein' still on the bed, went and fixed that sleepy dram, made it real strong, and when the young man came in to go to bed she handed it to him, made him drink it; but he kept it in his mouth and when she left he spit it out. Then he looked at that pillow and threw it off the bed. Laid down and closed his eyes. The woman she looked in at him to make sure he was asleep, then she let that girl in. She came in the room and saw him there with his eyes shut and her grief nearly killed her. She didn't know what she'd do. She came and sat on the edge of the bed and put her hand on his shoulder and started cryin':

"Three drops of blood I've shed for thee!
Three little babes I've born for thee!
Whitebear Whittington!—"

Well, time she called his name he opened his eyes
and turned to her, and then he knew her. So he put
his arms around her, and they went on to sleep.

The next morning that other woman came and
found the door locked and she was mad as time. And
after they got up, the young man he came and called
that woman's father, said, "Let's step outside. I want
a word with *you*."

So they went out and he told the man, says, "If
you had a lock and a key, and the key fitted the
lock perfect, and you lost that key and got a new
one; then you found the old key again, and it fitted
the lock much better than the new one—which key
would you keep?"

The old man answered him, says, "Why, I'd keep
the old one."

"Well," says the young man, "I found my old wife
last night and she suits me a lot better than your
daughter does, so you can just have her back."

So they left and got their three children and went
on home, and that spell on him was broke so he
never was a bear again, and they lived happy.

THE BLUE ROSE

By Maurice Baring from *The Art of the Story-Teller* by Marie L. Shedlock

THERE lived once upon a time in China a wise Emperor who had one daughter. His daughter was remarkable for her perfect beauty. Her feet were the smallest in the world; her eyes were long and slanting and bright as brown onyxes, and when you heard her laugh it was like listening to a tinkling stream or to the chimes of a silver bell. Moreover, the Emperor's daughter was as wise as she was beautiful, and she chanted the verse of the great poets better than anyone in the land. The Emperor was old in years; his son was married and had begotten a son; he was, therefore, quite happy with regard to the succession to the throne, but he wished before he died to see his daughter wedded to someone who should be worthy of her.

Many suitors presented themselves to the palace

as soon as it became known that the Emperor desired a son-in-law, but when they reached the palace they were met by the Lord Chamberlain, who told them that the Emperor had decided that only the man who found and brought back the blue rose should marry his daughter. The suitors were much puzzled by this order. What was the blue rose and where was it to be found? In all, a hundred and fifty suitors had presented themselves, and out of these, fifty at once put away from them all thought of winning the hand of the Emperor's daughter, since they considered the condition imposed to be absurd.

The other hundred set about trying to find the blue rose. One of them—his name was Ti-Fun-Ti—he was a merchant and was immensely rich, at once went to the largest shop in the town and said to the shopkeeper, "I want a blue rose, the best you have."

The shopkeeper, with many apologies, explained that he did not stock blue roses. He had red roses in profusion, white, pink, and yellow roses, but no blue roses. There had hitherto been no demand for the article.

"Well," said Ti-Fun-Ti, "you must get one for me. I do not mind how much money it costs, but I must have a blue rose."

The shopkeeper said he would do his best, but he feared it would be an expensive article and difficult

to procure. Another of the suitors, whose name I
have forgotten, was a warrior, and extremely brave;
he mounted his horse, and taking with him a hundred archers and a thousand horsemen, he marched
into the territory of the King of the Five Rivers, whom
he knew to be the richest king in the world and the
possessor of the rarest treasures, and demanded of
him the blue rose, threatening him with a terrible
doom should he be reluctant to give it up.

The King of the Five Rivers, who disliked soldiers
and had a horror of noise, physical violence, and
every kind of fuss (his bodyguard was armed solely
with fans and sunshades), rose from the cushions
on which he was lying when the demand was made,
and tinkling a small bell, said to the servant who
straightway appeared, "Fetch me the blue rose."

The servant retired and returned presently bear-
ing on a silken cushion a large sapphire which was
carved so as to imitate a full-blown rose with all its
petals.

"This," said the King of the Five Rivers, "is the
blue rose. You are welcome to it."

The warrior took it, and after making brief, sol-
dier-like thanks, he went straight back to the Emperor's palace, saying that he had lost no time in
finding the blue rose. He was ushered into the pres-

ence of the Emperor, who as soon as he heard the warrior's story and saw the blue rose which had been brought sent for his daughter and said to her: "This intrepid warrior has brought you what he claims to be the blue rose. Has he accomplished the quest?"

The Princess took the precious object in her hands and after examining it for a moment said: "This is not a rose at all. It is a sapphire; I have no need of precious stones." And she returned the stone to the warrior with many elegantly expressed thanks. And the warrior went away in discomfiture.

The merchant, hearing of the warrior's failure, was all the more anxious to win the prize. He sought the shopkeeper and said to him: "Have you got me the blue rose? I trust you have; because, if not, I shall most assuredy be the means of your death. My brother-in-law is chief magistrate, and I am allied by marriage to all the chief officials in the kingdom."

The shopkeeper turned pale and said: "Sir, give me three days and I will procure you the rose without fail." The merchant granted him the three days and went away. Now the shopkeeper was at his wits' end as to what to do, for he knew well there was no such thing as a blue rose. For two days he did nothing but moan and wring his hands, and on the third day he went to his wife and said, "Wife, we are ruined."

But his wife, who was a sensible woman, said: "Nonsense. If there is no such thing as a blue rose we must make one. Go to the chemist and ask him for a strong dye which will change a white rose into a blue one."

So the shopkeeper went to the chemist and asked for a dye, and the chemist gave him a bottle of red liquid, telling him to pick a white rose and to dip its stalk into the liquid and the rose would turn blue. The shopkeeper did as he was told; the rose turned into a beautiful blue and the shopkeeper took it to the merchant, who at once went with it to the palace saying that he had found the blue rose.

He was ushered into the presence of the Emperor, who as soon as he saw the blue rose sent for his daughter and said to her: "This wealthy merchant has brought you what he claims to be the blue rose. Has he accomplished the quest?"

The Princess took the flower in her hands and after examining it for a moment said: "This is a white rose; its stalk has been dipped in a poisonous dye and it has turned blue. Were a butterfly to settle upon it, it would die of the potent fume. Take it back. I have no need of a dyed rose." And she

returned it to the merchant with many elegantly expressed thanks.

The other ninety-eight suitors all sought in various ways for the blue rose. Some of them traveled all over the world seeking it; some of them sought the aid of wizards and astrologers, and one did not hesitate to invoke the help of the dwarfs that live underground; but all of them, whether they traveled in far countries or took counsel with wizards and demons or sat pondering in lonely places, failed to find the blue rose.

At last they all abandoned the quest except the Lord Chief Justice, who was the most skillful lawyer and statesman in the country. After thinking over the matter for several months he sent for the most famous artist in the country and said to him: "Make me a china cup. Let it be milk-white in colour and perfect in shape, and paint on it a rose, a blue rose."

The artist made obeisance and withdrew, and worked for two months at the Lord Chief Justice's cup. In two months' time it was finished, and the world has never seen such a beautiful cup, so perfect in symmetry, so delicate in texture, and the rose on it, the blue rose, was a living flower, picked in fairyland and floating on the rare milky surface of the porcelain. When the Lord Chief Justice saw it he gasped with surprise and pleasure, for he was a great lover of porcelain, and never in his life had he seen such a piece. He said to himself, "Without doubt the blue rose is here on this cup and nowhere else."

So, after handsomely rewarding the artist, he went to the Emperor's palace and said that he had brought the blue rose. He was ushered into the Emperor's presence, who as he saw the cup sent for his daughter and said to her: "This eminent lawyer has brought you what he claims to be the blue rose. Has he accomplished the quest?"

The Princess took the bowl in her hands and after examining it for a moment said: "This bowl is the most beautiful piece of china I have ever seen. If you are kind enough to let me keep it I will put it aside until I receive the blue rose, for so beautiful is it that no other flower is worthy to be put in it except the blue rose."

The Lord Chief Justice thanked the Princess for accepting the bowl with many elegantly turned phrases, and he went away in discomfiture.

After this there was no one in the whole country who ventured on the quest of the blue rose. It happened that not long after the Lord Chief Justice's attempt a strolling minstrel visited the kingdom of the Emperor. One evening he was playing his one-stringed instrument outside a dark wall. It was a summer's evening, and the sun had sunk in a glory of dusty gold, and in the violet twilight one or two stars were twinkling like spearheads. There was an incessant noise made by the croaking of frogs and the chatter of grasshoppers. The minstrel was singing a short song over and over again to a monotonous tune. The sense of it was something like this:

"I watched beside the willow trees
    The river, as the evening fell,
The twilight came and brought no breeze,
    Nor dew, nor water for the well.

"When from the tangled banks of grass
    A bird across the water flew,
And in the river's hard grey glass
    I saw a flash of azure blue."

As he sang he heard a rustle on the wall, and looking up, he saw a slight figure white against the twilight, beckoning to him. He walked along under the wall until he came to a gate, and there someone was waiting for him, and he was gently led into the shadow of a dark cedar tree. In the dim twilight he saw two bright eyes looking at him, and he understood their message. In the twilight a thousand meaningless nothings were whispered in the light of the stars, and the hours fled swiftly. When the east began to grow light, the Princess (for it was she) said it was time to go.

"But," said the minstrel, "to-morrow I shall come to the palace and ask for your hand."

"Alas!" said the Princess, "I would that were possible, but my father has made a foolish condition that only he may wed me who finds the blue rose."

"That is simple" said the minstrel. "I will find it." And they said good night to each other.

The next morning the minstrel went to the palace, and on his way he picked a common white rose from a wayside garden. He was ushered into the Emperor's presence, who sent for his daughter and said to her: "This penniless minstrel has brought you what he claims to be the blue rose. Has he accomplished the quest?"

The Princess took the rose in her hands and said: "Yes, this is without doubt the blue rose."

But the Lord Chief Justice and all who were present respectfully pointed out that the rose was a common white rose and not a blue one, and the objection was with many forms and phrases conveyed to the Princess.

"I think the rose is blue," said the Princess. "Perhaps you are all colour blind."

The Emperor, with whom the decision rested, decided that if the Princess thought the rose was blue it was blue, for it was well known that her perception was more acute than that of anyone else in the kingdom.

So the minstrel married the Princess, and they settled on the sea coast in a little-seen house with a garden full of white roses, and they lived happily for ever afterwards. And the Emperor, knowing that his daughter had made a good match, died in peace.

REFLECTIONS

From *Green Willow and Other Japanese Fairy Tales*
by Grace James

Long enough ago there dwelt within a day's journey of the city of Kioto a gentleman of simple mind and manners, but good estate. His wife, rest her soul, had been dead these many years, and the good man lived in great peace and quiet with his only son. They kept clear of women-kind, and knew nothing at all either of their winning or their bothering ways. They had good steady men-servants in their house, and never set eyes on a pair of long sleeves or a scarlet *obi* from morning till night.

The truth is that they were as happy as the day is long. Sometimes they laboured in the rice-fields. Other days they went a-fishing. In the spring, forth they went to admire the cherry flower or the plum, and later they set out to view the iris or the peony or the lotus, as the case might be. At these times they would drink a little *sake,* and twist their blue and white *tenegui* about their heads and be as jolly as you please, for there was no one to say them nay. Often enough they came home by lantern light. They wore their oldest clothes, and were mighty irregular at their meals.

But the pleasures of life are fleeting—more's the pity!—and presently the father felt old age creeping upon him.

One night, as he sat smoking and warming his hands over the charcoal, "Boy," says he, "it's high time you got married."

"Now the gods forbid!" cried the young man. "Father, what makes you say such terrible things? Or are you joking? You must be joking," he says.

"I'm not joking at all," says the father; "I never spoke a truer word, and that you'll know soon enough."

"But, father, I am mortally afraid of women."

"And am I not the same?" says the father. "I'm sorry for you, my boy."

"Then what for must I marry?" says the son.

"In the way of nature I shall die before long, and you'll need a wife to take care of you."

Now the tears stood in the young man's eyes when he heard this, for he was tender-hearted; but all he said was, "I can take care of myself very well."

"That's the very thing you cannot," says his father.

The long and short of it was that they found the young man a wife. She was young, and as pretty as a picture. Her name was Tassel, just that, or Fusa, as they say in her language.

After they had drunk down the "Three Times Three" together and so became man and wife, they stood alone, the young man looking hard at the girl. For the life of him he did not know what to say to her. He took a bit of her sleeve and stroked it with his hand. Still he said nothing and looked mighty foolish. The girl turned red, turned pale, turned red again, and burst into tears.

"Honourable Tassel, don't do that, for the dear gods' sake," says the young man.

"I suppose you don't like me," sobs the girl. "I suppose you don't think I'm pretty."

"My dear," he says, "you're prettier than the bean-flower in the field; you're prettier than the little bantam hen in the farm-yard; you're prettier than the rose carp in the pond. I hope you'll be happy with my father and me."

At this she laughed a little and dried her eyes. "Get on another pair of *hakama*," she says, "and give me those you've got on you; there's a great hole in them—I was noticing it all the time of the wedding!"

Well, this was not a bad beginning, and taking one

thing with another, they got on pretty well, though of course things were not as they had been in that blessed time when the young man and his father did not set eyes upon a pair of long sleeves or an *obi* from morning till night.

By and by, in the way of nature, the old man died. It is said he made a very good end, and left that in his strong-box which made his son the richest man in the country-side. But this was no comfort at all to the poor young man, who mourned his father with all his heart. Day and night he paid reverence to the tomb. Little sleep or rest he got, and little heed he gave to his wife, Mistress Tassel and her whimsies, or even to the delicate dishes she set before him. He grew thin and pale, and she, poor maid, was at her wits' end to know what to do with him. At last she said, "My dear, and how would it be if you were to go to Kioto for a little?"

"And what for should I do that?" he says.

It was on the tip of her tongue to answer, "To enjoy yourself," but she saw it would never do to say that.

"Oh," she says, "as a kind of a duty. They say every man that loves his country should see Kioto; and besides, you might give an eye to the fashions, so as to tell me what they are like when you get

home. My things," she says, "are sadly behind the
times! I'd like well enough to know what people are
wearing!"

"I've no heart to go to Kioto," says the young man,
"and if I had, it's the planting-out time of the rice,
and the thing's not to be done, so there's an end of
it."

All the same, after two days he bids his wife get
out his best *hakama* and *haouri,* and to make up his
bento for a journey. "I'm thinking of going to Kioto,"
he tells her.

"Well, I am surprised," says Mistress Tassel. "And
what put such an idea into your head, if I may ask?"

"I've been thinking it's a kind of duty," says the
young man.

"Oh, indeed," says Mistress Tassel to this, and
nothing more, for she had some grains of sense. And
the next morning as ever was she packs her husband
off bright and early for Kioto, and betakes herself
to some little matter of house cleaning she has on
hand.

The young man stepped out along the road, feel-
ing a little better in his spirits, and before long he
reached Kioto. It is likely he saw many things to wonder at. Amongst temples and palaces he went. He
saw castles and gardens, and marched up and down

fine streets of shops, gazing about him with his eyes wide open, and his mouth too, very like, for he was a simple soul.

At length, one fine day he came upon a shop full of metal mirrors that glittered in the sunshine.

"Oh, the pretty silver moons!" says the simple soul to himself. And he dared to come near and take up a mirror in his hand.

The next minute he turned as white as rice and sat him down on the seat in the shop door, still holding the mirror in his hand and looking into it.

"Why, father," he said, "how did you come here? You are not dead, then? Now the dear gods be praised for that! Yet I could have sworn— But no matter, since you are here alive and well. You are something pale still, but how young you look. You move your lips, father, and seem to speak, but I do not hear you. You'll come home with me, dear, and live with us just as you used to do? You smile, you smile, that is well."

"Fine mirrors, my young gentleman," said the shopman, "the best that can be made, and that's one of the best of the lot you have there. I see you are a judge."

The young man clutched his mirror tight and sat staring stupidly enough no doubt. He trembled. "How much?" he whispered. "Is it for sale?" He was in a fright lest his father should be snatched from him.

"For sale it is, indeed, most noble sir," said the shopman, "and the price is a trifle, only two *bu*. It's almost giving it away I am, as you'll understand."

"Two *bu*—only two *bu!* Now the gods be praised for this their mercy!" cried the happy young man. He smiled from ear to ear, and he had the purse out of his girdle and the money out of his purse in a twinkling.

Now it was the shopman who wished he had asked three *bu* or even five. All the same he put a good face upon it, and packed the mirror in a fine white box and tied it up with green cords.

"Father," said the young man, when he had got away with it, "before we set out for home we must buy some gauds for the young woman there, my wife, you know."

Now, for the life of him, he could not have told why, but when he came to his home the young man never said a word to Mistress Tassel about buying his old father for two *bu* in the Kioto shop. That was where he made his mistake, as things turned out.

She was as pleased as you like with her coral hair-pins, and her fine new *obi* from Kioto. "And I'm glad to see him so well and so happy," she said to herself; "but I must say he's been mighty quick to get over his sorrow after all. But men are just like children." As for her husband, unbeknown to her he took a bit of green silk from her treasure-box and spread it in the cupboard of the *toko no ma*. There he placed the mirror in its box of white wood.

Every morning early and every evening late, he went to the cupboard of the *toko no ma* and spoke with his father. Many a jolly talk they had and many a hearty laugh together, and the son was the happiest young man of all the country-side, for he was a simple soul.

But Mistress Tassel had a quick eye and a sharp ear, and it was not long before she marked her husband's new ways.

"What for does he go so often to the *toko no ma*," she asked herself, "and what has he got there? I should be glad enough to know." Not being one to suffer much in silence, she very soon asked her husband these same things.

He told her the truth, the good young man. "And now I have my dear old father home again, I'm as happy as the day is long," he says.

"H'm," she says.

"And wasn't two *bu* cheap," he says, "and wasn't it a strange thing altogether?"

"Cheap, indeed," says she, "and passing strange; and why, if I may ask," she says, "did you say nought of all this at the first?"

The young man grew red.

"Indeed, then, I cannot tell you, my dear," he says. "I'm sorry, but I don't know," and with that he went out to his work.

Up jumped Mistress Tassel the minute his back was turned, and to the *toko no ma* she flew on the wings of the wind and flung open the doors with a clang.

"My green silk for sleeve-linings!" she cried at once; "but I don't see any old father here, only a white wooden box. What can he keep in it?"

She opened the box quickly enough.

"What an odd flat shining thing!" she said and, taking up the mirror, looked into it.

For a moment she said nothing at all, but the great tears of anger and jealousy stood in her pretty eyes, and her face flushed from forehead to chin.

"A woman!" she cried, "a woman! So that is his secret! He keeps a woman in his cupboard. A woman, very young and very pretty—no, not pretty at all, but she thinks herself so. A dancing-girl from Kioto, I'll be bound; ill-tempered too—her face is scarlet; and oh, how she frowns, nasty little spit-fire. Ah, who could have thought it of him? Ah, it's a miserable girl I am—and I've cooked his *daikon* and mended his *hakama* a hundred times. Oh! oh! oh!"

With that, she threw the mirror into its case, and slammed-to the cupboard door upon it. Herself she flung upon the mats, and cried and sobbed as if her heart would break.

In comes her husband.

"I've broken the thong of my sandal," says he, "and I've come to— But what in the world?" and in an instant he was down on his knees beside Mistress Tassel doing what he could to comfort her, and to get her face up from the floor where she kept it.

"Why, what is it, my own darling?" says he.

"*Your* own darling!" she answers very fierce through her sobs; and "I want to go home," she cries.

"But, my sweet, you are at home, and with your own husband."

"Pretty husband!" she says, "and pretty going-on, with a woman in the cupboard! A hateful, ugly woman that thinks herself beautiful; and she has *my* green sleeve-linings there with her to boot."

"Now, what's all this about women and sleeve-linings? Sure you wouldn't grudge poor old father that little green rag for his bed? Come, my dear, I'll buy you twenty sleeve-linings."

At that she jumped to her feet and fairly danced with rage.

"Old father! old father! old father!" she screamed; "am I a fool or a child? I saw the woman with my own eyes."

The poor young man didn't know whether he was on his head or his heels. "Is it possible that my father is gone?" he said, and he took the mirror from the *toko no ma.*

"That's well; still the same old father that I bought for two *bu.* You seem worried, father; nay, then, smile as I do. There, that's well."

Mistress Tassel came like a little fury and snatched the mirror from his hand. She gave but one look into it and hurled it to the other end of the room. It made such a clang against the woodwork that servants and neighbours came rushing in to see what was the matter.

"It is my father," said the young man. "I bought him in Kioto for two *bu.*"

"He keeps a woman in the cupboard who has stolen my green sleeve-linings," sobbed the wife.

After this there was a great to-do. Some of the neighbours took the man's part and some the woman's, with such a clatter and chatter and noise as never was; but settle the thing they could not, and none of them would look into the mirror, because they said it was bewitched.

They might have gone on the way they were till doomsday, but that one of them said, "Let us ask the Lady Abbess, for she is a wise woman." And off they all went to do what they might have done sooner.

The Lady Abbess was a pious woman, the head of a convent of holy nuns. She was the great one at prayers and meditations and at mortifyings of the flesh, and she was the clever one, none the less, at human affairs. They took her the mirror, and she held it in her hands and looked into it for a long time. At last she spoke:

"This poor woman," she said, touching the mirror, "for it's as plain as daylight that it is a woman—this poor woman was so troubled in her mind at the disturbance that she caused in a quiet house that she had taken vows, shaved her head, and become a holy nun. Thus she is in her right place here. I will keep her, and instruct her in prayers and meditations. Go you home, my children; forgive and forget, be friends."

Then all the people said, "The Lady Abbess is the wise woman."

And she kept the mirror in her treasure.

Mistress Tassel and her husband went home hand in hand.

"So I was right, you see, after all," she said.

"Yes, yes, my dear," said the simple young man, "of course. But I was wondering how my old father would get on at the holy convent. He was never much of a one for religion."

THE LIGHT PRINCESS

by George MacDonald, edited by the compiler

NCE upon a time there lived a king and a queen who had no children. So the king made up his mind to be cross with the queen about it, and it was more than he deserved, therefore, when at last she gave him a daughter—as lovely a little princess as ever cried.

The day grew near when the princess must be christened. The king wrote all the invitations with his own hand, and of course somebody was forgotten.

Unfortunately the somebody was the Princess Makemnoit. She was a sour, old spiteful creature. Her face was as full of wrinkles as a dried-up prune. Her forehead was as large as all the rest of her face and hung over it like a precipice. When she was angry, her little eyes flashed blue. When she hated anyone, they shone yellow and green. What they looked like when she loved anybody I do not know, for I never heard of her loving anybody but herself, and it took her a long time to manage even that.

What made it highly imprudent of the king to forget her was: she was a witch. She could beat all the wicked witches in wickedness and all the clever ones in cleverness. When she bewitched anybody, he stayed bewitched.

After waiting and waiting in vain for an invitation to the princess's christening, the Princess Makemnoit made up her mind at last to go without one and make the whole family miserable—like the witch she was.

So she put on her best gown, went to the palace, was kindly received by the happy king (who forgot that he had forgotten her), and took her place in the procession to the royal chapel. When they were all gathered around the christening font, the Princess Makemnoit contrived to get next to it and throw something into the water. Then, when the water was sprinkled on the little princess's head, the old witch turned round in her place three times and muttered under her breath:

> "Light of spirit, by my charms,
> Light of body, every part,
> Never weary human arms—
> Only crush thy parents' hearts!"

Those who were standing beside the Princess Makemnoit thought she had lost her wits and was repeating some foolish nursery rhyme, but a shudder went through each one of them notwithstanding. At the same time the nurse who was holding the little princess gave a start and a smothered cry, for suddenly she could not feel the baby in her arms any more. The baby, however, began to laugh and crow.

The mischief was done. The witch had deprived the little princess of her gravity.

When the strange fact came to be known, there was a terrible commotion in the palace. The occasion of its discovery by the king was naturally a repetition of the nurse's experience: he felt no weight when the little princess was laid in his arms. Astonished, he bounced her up in the air, but not down again; for the princess simply flew from his arms, ascended to the ceiling, and there remained floating in perfect comfort and satisfaction. The king stood staring in speechless amazement. At last, turning to the queen, he stammered: "She *can't* be ours, Queen!"

Now the queen was just as horror-struck as the king, but she was cleverer than he and had begun already to suspect what had happened.

"Of course she is ours," answered the queen, "but we ought to have taken better care of her at the

christening. People who were not invited ought not to have been present."

"Oh, ho!" said the king, tapping his forehead with his forefinger, "I see it all. The Princess Makemnoit has bewitched our daughter."

"That's just what I said," answered the queen.

Then the king sent John, the page, to fetch the throne-steps. The throne-steps were brought and set upon the dining-table and John climbed to the top of them, but he still could not reach the little princess who lay like a baby-laughter-cloud in the air.

"Here, take the tongs, John," said the king and handed them up.

Now, John could just catch the floating tail of the baby's long dress, and so the little princess was handed down by the fire tongs.

The princess was watched carefully; yet it would take me a long time to tell you all the odd things that happened to her because she had no gravity. But there never was a baby in a house, or a palace, that kept the household in such constant good humour. At least below stairs. If it was not easy for her nurses to hold onto her, at least she made neither their arms nor their hearts ache. And she was so nice to play ball with! If you heard peals of laughter from the kitchen and went down there, you were

sure to find Jane and Thomas, and Robert and Susan,
playing at ball with the little princess. She *was* the
ball and away she went, flying from one to the other,
screeching with laughter. And the servants loved
the ball itself better than the game. Of course they
had to take some care how they threw her lest she
fly into the fire, or up the chimney, or out the window. But none of these accidents had happened as
yet, and there was positively no danger of letting
the princess fall. They might throw her down, or
put her down, or hold her down, but they could
not let her fall down.

But above stairs it was different.

One day the king went into his counting-house
and counted out his money. The operation gave him
no pleasure.

"To think," said he to himself, "that every one of
these gold sovereigns weighs a quarter of an ounce,
and my real, live, flesh-and-blood daughter weighs
nothing at all!"

And he hated his gold sovereigns as they lay with
broad smiles of self-satisfaction all over their yellow
faces.

The queen was in the parlor, eating bread and
honey, but at the second mouthful she burst out
crying and could not swallow it. The king heard
her sobbing, clashed his gold sovereigns into his

money-box, clapped his crown on his head, and rushed into the parlor.

The queen looked so rueful that the king took her in his arms, and they sat down to consult.

"Can you bear this," asked the king, "having a daughter who is light-headed, light-minded, and too light-hearted?"

"No, I can't," said the queen.

"Well, what's to be done?" said the king.

"I'm sure I don't know," said the queen, "but might you not try an apology to the Princess Makemnoit?"

So the next morning the king went to the house of the old witch and, making a very humble apology, begged her to undo the spell. But the princess declared, with a grave face, that she knew nothing at all about it. Her eyes, however, shone pink, which was a sign that she was happy.

The king returned disconsolate, and now it was the queen's turn to comfort him. "We will just wait till she is older. She may then be able to suggest something herself. She will know at least how she feels and can explain things to us."

And so the princess laughed and grew—not fat, but plump and tall. She reached the age of seventeen without having fallen into anything worse than the chimney. Nor, thoughtless as she was, had she done anything worse than laugh at everybody and everything that came in her way. Only in her laugh there was something missing—a certain tone, depending on the possibility of sorrow perhaps. She never smiled.

At last the king and queen resolved to talk to the princess; but although she tried to behave herself with dignity, she was presently rolling about the floor in gales of laughter at their questions.

"Would you not like to be able to walk like other people?" asked the king.

"No, indeed, I should think not," said the princess. "You only crawl. You are such slow coaches!"

"Is there nothing you wish for?" said the king.

"Oh, yes, dear papa!" said the princess. "I would like to be tied to the end of a string—a very long string indeed—and be flown like a kite. Oh, such fun! I would rain rose-water, and hail sugar-plums, and snow whipped cream, and—and—and—"

A fit of laughter checked the princess, and the king, seeing that nothing but nonsense could be got out of her, rang the bell and sent her away with two of her ladies-in-waiting.

Now the palace where the princess lived was built on the shores of the loveliest lake in the world. One summer evening, during the carnival of the country, the princess was taken out on the lake by the king and queen in the royal barge. They were accompanied by many of the courtiers in a fleet of little boats. In the middle of the lake the princess wanted to get into the lord chancellor's barge, for his daughter, who was a great favorite with the princess, was in the barge with her father. Now the king rarely made light of his daughter's misfortune; yet, happening to be in a particularly good humor, as the barges drew together, he caught up the princess to throw her into the chancellor's barge. Unfortunately the king lost his balance and, dropping into the bottom of the barge, lost his hold of his daughter as well; not, however, before imparting to her the downward tendency of his own person, though in a somewhat different direction; for, as the king fell into the boat, the princess fell into the lake. With a burst of delighted laughter she disappeared into the water. A cry of horror went up from the boats. Half the men were under water in a moment; but they had all, one after another, come up to the surface again for breath when—tinkle, tinkle, babble, and gush! came the princess's laugh over the water from far away. There she was, swimming like a swan. Nor would she come out for king or queen, chancellor or daughter.

After that, the passion of the princess's life was to

get into the water, and she was always better be-
haved and more beautiful the more she had of it.
The root of her preference was, no doubt, that the
moment she got into the lake she recovered the
gravity of which she had been so wickedly deprived
by the Princess Makemnoit. Summer and winter it
was quite the same; only she could not stay so long
in the water when they had to break the ice to let
her in! Any day, from morning to evening in summer,
she might be seen—a streak of white in the blue
water—lying as still as the shadow of a cloud, or
shooting along like a dolphin. She would have been
in the lake of a night too, if she could have managed
it, for the balcony of her window overhung a deep
pool in it. But there was the sad difficulty of getting
into it. If she gave herself a push toward the water,
the slightest gust of wind might blow her away,
suspend her from a tree branch by her nightgown,
and leave her there to dangle until someone came
to fetch her down.

"Oh! if I only had my gravity," said the princess,
"I would flash off this balcony like a long white sea-
bird, headlong into the dear wetness." This was the
only time the princess wished to be like other people.

So remarkable were the effects of the water on the
princess that two professors in the king's College of
Metaphysicians, Hum-Drum and Kopy-Keck, recom-

mended that the king bury the princess alive for
three years. If the water did her so much good, they
said, the earth would do her even more. Fortunately
the king would not give his consent to this. Then,
they argued, if external water did the princess so
much good, water from an inner source might work
a perfect cure. Perhaps if the poor afflicted princess
could by any means be made to cry, she might re-
cover her lost gravity. But how was this to be brought
about? To make the princess cry was as impossible
as to make her weigh. So anxious was the king that
the suggestion should have a fair trial that he put
himself in a rage one day and, rushing up to the
princess's room, gave her a dreadful whipping. Yet
not a tear would flow. The princess looked grave
and her laughter sounded uncommonly like screaming—that was all.

It must have been about this time that the son of
a king, who lived a thousand miles away, set out to
look for the daughter of a queen. He traveled far
and wide, but as surely as he found a princess, he
found some fault in her.

One day the prince lost his retinue in a great
forest. It was getting late and there was no one to
direct him, but presently he came upon a footpath.
He followed along it in the gathering darkness until

he came to the shore of a lake. Suddenly he paused and listened. Strange sounds came across the water. It was, in fact, the princess laughing. Now there was always something odd in the princess's laugh, you will remember, and perhaps that is why the prince mistook it for screaming. Looking over the lake, he saw something white in the water, and in an instant he had torn off his tunic, kicked off his sandals, and plunged in the lake. He soon reached the white object and found it was a maiden.

Now I cannot tell how it came about—whether the princess pretended to be drowning or whether the prince really frightened her—but certainly he brought her to shore in a fashion disgraceful to a swimmer, and more nearly drowned than she had ever expected to be.

At the place to which the prince brought the princess the bank was only a foot or two above the lake, so he gave her a strong lift out of the water to lay her on the bank. And away went the princess up into the air, scolding and screaming.

When the prince saw her rise in the air, he thought he must have been bewitched and mistaken a swan for a maiden. He stood in the water staring, forgetting to get out, until the princess disappeared in the tree tops. Then he scrambled ashore and went in the same direction. The princess meanwhile had caught hold of a cone on a lofty pine to check her flight, and with the help of cones and branches she managed to get down to the ground. She was just stepping out of the tree when the prince arrived below it. She caught hold of him and began to scold.

"I shall tell my papa on you. Yes, I will. What business had you to pull me down out of the water and throw me to the bottom of the air? I never did you any harm. I don't believe you have any brains, and that is a worse loss than your wretched gravity!"

Now the prince knew that he had come upon the bewitched princess he had heard about—and had offended her. But before he could think what to say next, the princess ordered him angrily:

"Put me up at once."

"Put you up where, my beauty?" asked the prince.

"Up in the water, you stupid!" answered the princess.

"Come, then," said the prince.

Now they came upon the lake at quite another part where the bank was at least twenty-five feet high, and when they reached the edge, the prince turned to the princess.

"How am I to put you in?" he asked.

"That is your business," snapped the princess. "You took me out, now put me in again."

"Very well," said the prince, and catching her up

in his arms, he sprang from the rock. The princess had just time to give one delighted shriek of laughter before the water closed over them. When she came to the surface, she found that for a moment or two she could not even laugh, for she had gone down with such a rush that her breath was quite gone.

"How do you like falling in?" asked the prince.

"Is that what you call *falling in?*" panted the princess. "It seemed to me like going up; but it is the most delightful fun I ever had in my life. I never fell before. I wish I could learn. To think I am the only person in my father's kingdom who can't fall!"

"I shall be most happy to fall in with you anytime you like," offered the prince, for he had fallen in love with the princess when he fell in the lake with her.

And away they went then, swimming and diving and floating until the hour was late and the princess had to return to the palace. Then the prince found a sort of cave in the rock on the shore of the lake where he could see the light in the princess's room. He made himself a bed of withered leaves and lay down, too tired for hunger to keep him awake. And all night long he dreamed he was swimming with the princess.

Night after night the prince and princess met and swam about in the dark clear lake. The prince soon found out that while in the water the princess was very like other people. She was not so forward in her questions or pert in her replies. Neither did she laugh so much, and when she did laugh, it was more gently. She seemed altogether more modest and maidenly in the water than out of it. But when the prince began to talk to her of love, she looked a little puzzled as if she were trying to understand—and then she laughed.

Now it came to the ears of the old Princess Makemnoit that the princess was finding more pleasure in the lake than any one else had out of it, and she went into a rage. "I will soon set all right," she said. "I will not be cheated of my revenge."

Then she went to an old chest and, opening it, took out what looked like a piece of dried seaweed. This she threw into a tub of water. Then she threw some powder into the water and stirred it with her bare arm. Next she set the tub aside and took from the chest a huge bunch of one hundred rusty keys that clattered in her shaking hands. Then she sat down and proceeded to oil them all. Before she had finished, out from the tub came the head and half the body of a great gray snake. It grew out of the tub till it reached the princess, laid its head upon her shoulder, and gave a low hiss in her ear. The old witch started—but with joy. She drew all of the snake out of the tub and wound it round her body.

Then she took the keys and went down to her cellar. Locking the door behind her, she descended a few steps into the cellar and, crossing it, unlocked another door into a dark, narrow passage. She locked this also behind her and descended a few more steps. If anyone had followed the witch, he would have heard her unlock exactly one hundred doors and descend a few steps after unlocking each. When she had unlocked the last, she entered a vast cave, the roof of which was supported by huge natural pillars of rock. Now this roof was the under side of the bottom of the lake.

Then the witch untwined the snake from her body —the White Snake of Darkness it was called—and held it high above her. She began to walk round and round the cavern, coming nearer to the center with every circuit, while the snake described the same path over the roof that she did over the floor. Round and round the cavern they went till at last the snake made a sudden dart and clung to the roof with its mouth.

"That's right, my beauty!" cried the old witch. "Drain it dry!"

She let it go, left it hanging, and sat down on a great stone with her black cat by her side. Then she began to knit and mutter words of black magic and evil sorcery. The snake hung from the roof of the cavern; the cat stood with his back arched and his tail like a piece of cable; and the old witch sat and knitted and muttered to herself. Seven days and seven nights they remained thus. Then suddenly the serpent dropped from the roof as if exhausted and shrivelled up till it was again like a piece of dried seaweed. The witch started to her feet, picked it up, put it in her pocket, and then looked up at the roof. One drop of water trembled on the spot where the snake had been sucking. When the witch saw that she turned and fled. Up the steps she sped, through the one hundred doors, till she arrived in her own cellar. Only then did she stop and listen to the rushing of the water which she could hear distinctly through all the hundred doors.

But this was not enough. The lake would be too long in disappearing. So the next night, with the last shred of the dying moon in the sky, she took some of the water in which she had revived the White Snake of Darkness, put it in a bottle, and set forth. Before morning she had made the entire circuit of the lake, casting into every stream as she crossed it some of the water out of her bottle. When she had finished the circuit, she flung what was left of the water toward the moon. Thereupon every spring in the country ceased to bubble, every stream ceased to flow, and there was no sound of falling water to be heard along the borders of the lake.

The lake began to sink away, slowly vanishing. The tops of rocks that had never been seen till now began to appear, far down in the clear water. Before long they were dry in the sun.

One night when the princess was diving with the prince she began to suspect that the lake was not so deep as it used to be. She saw that the banks were too dry and that the grass on the shore and the trailing plants on the rocks were withering away. She had marks made along the borders of the lake and examined them each day till at last the horrible suspicion became a certain fact: the lake was slowly sinking away.

The poor princess nearly went out of the little mind she had. It was terrible for her to see the lake, which she loved more than any living thing, disappear before her eyes. She could not bear to swim in it any more and began to pine away. Her life seemed bound up with the lake, and ever as the lake sank, the princess seemed to sink too. People said she would not live an hour after the lake was gone. As for the prince—he was forgotten.

And the lake went on sinking. Small slimy spots began to appear which glittered steadily amidst the changeful shine of the water. These grew to broad patches of mud which widened and spread. At length the lake was all but gone; only a few of the deepest pools remained.

Now it happened one day that some children found themselves on the brink of one of these pools in the very center of the lake. Looking down into the water, they saw at the bottom something that shone yellow in the sun. One of the boys jumped in and dived for it. It was a plate of gold covered with writing. They took it to the king, for the writing said: "If the lake should disappear, find the hole through which the water runs and stop it up. But it will be useless to try to stop it by any ordinary means. The body of a living man can alone staunch the flow. The man must give himself of his own will and the lake must take his life as it fills."

No time was to be lost, for the princess was lying motionless on her bed. The king caused the contents of the plate of gold to be proclaimed throughout the country.

No one came forward to give his life for the princess. No one—except the prince.

"Upon one condition," said the prince. "Since I must on no account die before I am fairly drowned and the waiting will be hard, the princess, your daughter, must go with me, feed me with her own hands, and look at me now and then to comfort me. As soon as the water is up to my eyes, she may go and be happy and forget her poor prince."

The king agreed to the condition and then ordered out his guards to find the hole in the lake. In an hour or so it was discovered. It was in the middle of a great flat stone in the very pool where the golden plate had been found. It was a three-cornered hole of no great size. There was water all round the stone, but very little was flowing through the hole.

When the princess heard that a man had offered to die for her, she jumped from her bed, feeble as she was, and danced about the room for joy. She did not care who the man was; that was nothing to her. The hole wanted stopping, and if only a man would do, why, take one. In an hour or two everything was ready. The servants carried the princess across to the stone, where a little boat had been placed for her. They laid her on cushions, placed in the boat wines and fruits, and stretched a canopy over all.

In a few minutes the prince appeared. "Here I am," said the prince. "Put me in."

But how was he to be put in? The golden plate contained no instructions on this point. The prince looked at the hole and saw but one way. He put both his legs into it, sitting on the stone, and stooping forward, covered the corner that remained open with his two hands. In this position he would die.

Then the people went away and left the prince and the princess alone. Presently a little wave flowed over the stone and wetted one of the prince's knees. Again a wavelet, and another, and another flowed over the stone and wetted both the prince's knees; yet he neither spoke nor moved. Two—three—four hours passed in this way, and then suddenly the princess shouted with joy: "I'm afloat! I'm afloat!" And the little boat swung free and bumped gently against the stone where the prince was sitting.

"A glass of wine and a biscuit, please," said the prince, very humbly.

"With all my heart," said the princess and held the wine out to him.

"Ah! you must feed me. I dare not move my hands. The water would run away directly."

And the princess fed him with bits of biscuit and sips of wine.

The sun went down and the moon rose, and wave after wave the waters were rising up the prince's body. They were up to his waist now. The princess sat and looked at him and fed him from time to time. The waters rose and rose. The moon rose higher and higher too and shone full on the face of the dying prince. The water was up to his neck now.

"Will you kiss me, princess?" said the prince feebly.

And the princess kissed him with a long, sweet, cold kiss.

The prince did not speak again. The princess gave him some wine for the last time: he was past eating. The water rose and rose. It touched his chin. It touched his lower lip. It touched between his lips. He shut them hard to keep it out. The princess began to feel strange. It touched his upper lip. He breathed through his nostrils. The princess looked wild. It covered his nostrils. The princess's eyes looked scared and shone strangely in the moonlight. The prince's head fell back; the water closed over it, and the bubbles of his last breath came up through the water. The princess gave a shriek and sprang into the lake.

She laid hold first of one leg, and then of the other, and pulled and tugged, but she could not move either. She stopped to take breath, and that made her think that the prince could not get any breath and she was frantic. She got hold of him and held his head above the water, but it was of no use, for he was past breathing.

Then love and water brought back all the princess's strength. She got under the water and pulled and pulled with her whole might till at last she got one of the prince's legs out of the hole. The other easily followed. How she got him into the boat she never could tell, but when she did, she seized the oars, kept herself as steady as best she could, and rowed and rowed round rocks, and over shallows, and through mud till she got to the landing-stairs of the palace. By this time her people were on the shore, for they had heard her shriek. She made them carry the prince to her own room and lay him in her bed and light a fire and send for her old nurse.

"But the lake, your highness!" said the chancellor.

"Go and drown yourself in it!" answered the princess, and this was the last rudeness she was ever guilty of.

So the princess and the old nurse were left with the prince. The nurse was a wise woman and knew what to do. Just as the sun rose, the prince opened his eyes.

And when the princess saw this, she burst into tears and *fell* on the floor. There she lay for an hour, and her tears never ceased. All the pent-up crying of her life was spent now. And a rain came on such as had never been seen in that country. The sun shone all the time, and the great drops which fell straight to the earth shone likewise. The palace was in the heart of a rainbow, and the lake was full from shore to shore.

When the princess's tears had stopped, she tried

to rise from the floor but only tumbled down again. When the prince heard her, he sat up in bed and shouted with delight: "My princess has got back her gravity." And so she had.

There was rejoicing all over the country that rainy day. The king divided the money in his box, and the queen the honey in her pot, among all the children. The prince taught the princess to walk with gravity, and there was such jubiliation as was never heard of before.

The water undermined the house of old Princess Makemnoit, and it fell in during the night, burying her in its ruins, and there she lies to this day, and her black cat and the White Snake of Darkness lie with her.

So the prince and the princess lived and were happy; they had crowns of gold, and clothes of gold, and shoes of leather, and children of boys and girls, not one of whom was ever known, on the most critical occasion, to lose the smallest atom of his or her due proportion of gravity.

AFTERWORD

This book, as the title page says, is especially for girls. I hope those who read it will take a special feminine delight in the stories I have included in it. I have told these stories to many girls, and the telling and the listening have been a shared pleasure.

Perhaps other storytellers may find this a useful sampler when they, too, need a story for girls.